WORRY BEADS

THE BIG UNEASY 4

PAULINE BAIRD JONES

ISBN: 978-1-942583-80-6

❀ Created with Vellum

WORRY BEADS: THE BIG UNEASY 4

Laura Baker has seen a lot during her job as a New Orleans EMT. She has responded to just about every type of emergency known to man. An unexpected act of kindness during one call puts her on the news—and her life and heart at risk.

Archie Gunn receives an unexpected tip that sends him to the beautiful and mysterious city of New Orleans. His trip opens up more than he expects – and a bayou full of danger. There is a lot going on in New Orleans and it isn't all good times and Mardi Gras.

Download the latest installment of The Big Uneasy series and discover what happens in New Orleans can be downright deadly!

1

THE SMELL in the alley was not subtle, but was sadly familiar. At least it was cooler this time of year, so the smell wasn't getting amped up by the heat. Even if it had been chilled, Laura Baker would be taking whatever she was kneeling in home with her. Garbage, urine, and of course, blood. Lots of blood. He lay where the car had tossed him, legs and arms bent at angles they'd never been meant to go. And because it was New Orleans, jazz played in the distance, the sound carried in by the cool January night air, while their emergency lights pulsed across the scene.

She was working on getting his vitals. LaFon was still trying to find a vein for the cannula.

Guy hadn't moved since they got there. Based on his vital signs, he wouldn't be—

His lids lifted, the fog in his eyes clearing just enough for him to focus on Laura.

His blue lips moved. "You a real blonde?"

Her lips twitched.

"Would you believe me if I said I was?" she asked, her gaze

holding his while her hands continued their all too familiar task.

"I would," LaFon said, a white grin cutting across his dark face.

"Always liked blondes," their victim muttered. The hand nearest her twitched, shifting in the pile of she-didn't-want-to-know-what it was. He winced, the effort adding more gray to his face, but he managed to lift his hand enough so she could see he held some Mardi Gras beads.

She almost sighed. Orleanians did like their beads, but she wasn't going to show him something to get them.

"Take them. Pretty girl should have...beads." Air bubbles popped in the blood that oozed out with each word.

She met LaFon's gaze and he half shrugged. "Make him feel better, girl," he advised.

Laura gingerly extracted the strand from fingers almost as twisted as limbs and held it up. It was strung with what was probably the usual fake pearls and a huge bobble hung off the Krewe badge. With a smile hiding her sigh, she slung it around her neck. He was dying and she'd had worse things on her uniform.

"How does it look?" she asked, giving him a sultry smile, even as she returned to the futile task of trying to save his life.

The edges of his mouth moved. "Hang on...bring... you...luck..."

The beads hadn't brought him luck, but she smiled again and thanked him. "I'll hang on to them," she promised. "For luck."

The man's gaze slid sideways, as if looking to see if anyone was near. The beat cops were keeping the small crowd back. Most people were a couple of streets over on Bourbon Street. The distant music changed to something slower and very jazzy.

"Ogre..." The effort exhausted him and his eyes closed. "Hunt...ogre..." he said again.

"We'll do what we can," she said, trying to sound reassuring.

"Bay..."

"Bay?" Laura tried not to make it a question, hoping that her calm tone would reassure him.

"Ba...by..."

Her gaze flicked to LaFon who shrugged. It wasn't unusual to call someone baby around here, but the way he said it was neither the affectionate or the creepy version. More like...scared.

"Baby."

His lids flickered, lifting enough for him to see her again. "Pretty girl...careful..."

"I'm always careful."

Suddenly his eyes opened wide. "Treasure."

He said the word clearly and she shot LaFon a startled look. Then the man's eyes dimmed, light fading from them as he flatlined.

No way to do CPR on a crushed chest. LaFon shook his head, rubbing his forearm against his forehead in a weary gesture.

"He was gone before we got here."

Laura started to take the beads off, but it felt wrong to toss them aside, no matter how slimy and hideous—and she had promised—so she flung them around so they lay against her back, out of her way, and then signaled the uniform keeping the crowds at bay.

"He's gone."

"He say anything about who hit him?"

"An ogre," LaFon said, with a tired grin.

She started to collect their equipment. The uniform spoke into the walkie-talkie on his shoulder, then crouched to help. Since he didn't know what he was doing, he was more hinder than helper. She handed him the body bag.

He held it up, gulped, and handed it on to LaFon. "Baker, right?"

Laura sighed. When you had as many siblings as she did... she nodded. "Yeah."

"Was at a shooting with your brother a couple of hours ago."

She didn't ask which brother because she figured she knew. Alex had managed to get back on the day shift and stay there for an extended period. He did have a big incentive to stay home at night now that he and Nell had tied the knot.

"Long day," Laura said. She glanced at her watch. Speaking of long days, theirs had inched past the twelve-hour mark about half an hour ago. The cop helped them shift the body onto the stretcher. She reached for one of their cases, but the uniform beat her to it.

"Thanks." Laura managed a smile for him.

He must be new if he was moving on her, especially after meeting Alex. She gave him a quick glance. Not bad, but young, too young to stand up to her seven brothers. That would take someone with some big brass ones. She tried to imagine what that guy would be like, other than as annoying as her brothers. Of course, could just be a guy being friendly. She was not exactly hit-on worthy covered in blood and garbage.

He lifted the case into the spot she indicated.

"I'll see you around," he said, a bit wistfully.

She glanced back and gave him a wave, noting the television news camera near the street. The crowd was starting to thin on either side of the small news crew, and her attention was caught by a tall, thin man standing half in shadow. As if he sensed her attention, his head turned her way. His flat, cold gaze made her skin crawl. Then he stepped back, melting into the crowd. Though the glimpse had been brief, she'd know him if she saw him again. And as the daughter of a cop, she hoped she never would. Crap people didn't always telegraph their crappiness, but this guy, well, what he telegraphed wasn't anything close to nice.

She realized the cameras had started to track their direction again, and she turned back to loading and getting away fast. She and LaFon each closed a rear door, then trotted around to their respective sides of the ambulance and clambered in. She heaved a sigh of relief as they pulled away.

The necklace dug into her back so she lifted it off, stared at it without seeing it for a minute, then shoved it in her pocket. Their hit and run wouldn't care now.

———

Laura Baker not only had seven brothers, she also had five sisters, all of them varying degrees of blonde and okay looking. They should have all had mildly active dating lives. But the seven brothers—and their ex-cop dad—loomed over the Baker girls like Stonehenge. Alex's partner, Logan Ferris, had managed to break into the circle with Hannah, but he was going to have to put a ring on it to get anything. He was being closely monitored for any signs he'd lost that hungry look of longing.

Alex might have hoped the rules didn't apply to him and Nell, but she'd had a different kind of Family—the criminally organized type—watching them, so he'd done the only thing he could do. He'd married the girl. Nell was one of them now, for better or worse.

Laura bent to wash her face and felt the unyielding mass of the Mardi Gras beads inside her jacket pocket. She extracted it from the pocket. The strand was longer and chunkier than the beads she was used to. And it was even nastier in the bathroom light than they'd been in the street light. She almost tossed them in the trash, but the memory of the look in the dying man's eyes —and his words, particularly the last word—stopped her. *Trea-*

sure. She dangled the string between two fingers. They did look to be the "good" kind of beads, the ones you usually had to show your boobs to get. Of course, if she wore them, everyone would think she'd lifted her shirt for them.

She hesitated again, then ran some water in the bowl and gave them a good cleaning with some disinfectant hand soap. She patted them dry with paper towels and held them up again. Cleaned up, the beads weren't totally awful. That big blue stone that dangled below a Krewe badge that looked like it had been carved out of wood. The blue stone caught the light, flickering with a muted blue fire. She lifted it closer so she could study the Krewe badge. She didn't recognize it. The beads looked aged, almost like real pearls. Back in the day, Mardi Gras strands used to be made out of glass, she recalled. These looked aged enough —or had been faked to be aged, she decided. Granted their victim had been tossed in the garbage, but there'd been something seedy about him that did not indicate a lot of prosperity.

She rubbed the beads between her fingers, her daughter-of-a-cop's brain wondering if there was a connection between a hit and run and this strand. *Treasure?* What had he meant by that? And don't forget the ogre or the scary baby, she reminded herself. Where treasure was concerned one should never forget the ogre, though the baby was a new twist. She half smiled, then frowned at the strand. Could they be valuable?

How could she know? She came from blue-collar stock, the kind without family jewels. She hesitated once more, then wrapped the bead string in more paper towels and tucked it in the pocket of her light jacket. She released the clips holding her hair up, feeling tension releasing as her hair fell around her shoulders.

Outside, dawn was just edging over the city, spilling light on glass-sided buildings and the Greater New Orleans bridge. She rubbed her tired face as her car pulled up with her brother

Frank at the wheel. She clambered in next to him, arching a weary brow in his direction.

"Couple more days in the shop. Thanks for the borrow."

He looked back, pulled into the street, and then relaxed enough to slant a glance at her. "Must have been a slow news night. I saw your backside on TV at eleven. Not the lead, but right after it."

"At least they got my best side." One thing all the Baker girls had learned growing up with seven older brothers, show no reaction or the hits would ramp up. She slid down until she could rest her head against the door and gazed out at the passing city through sleep blurred eyes.

"What was with the nasty beads?"

She half frowned and glanced at Frank, but he was looking at the road. Which he should be. How did he know—the news camera. Apparently, the beads had also made the local news. Yay. "My reward for being a real blonde."

He glanced at her with a quick grin. She saw the next question in his eyes and said, "Don't—" She looked ahead with a sigh. "He didn't make it."

"Sorry." His tone was the one men used in the face of emotion.

That was one of the advantages of being an EMS. She could kill the conversation faster than her dad.

As the second youngest, she'd kind of hoped it would get easier as siblings peeled off to their own places, their own lives. Sadly, she'd seen no sign the brothers had lost interest in any of the sisters' dating lives. And she'd lost the toss for who had to move back in with their dad when Alex moved in with his wife. Speaking of which—she saw the house come into view as Frank turned the corner. At least she didn't have to look for a parking space, something that was almost impossible to find this time of day.

The car jerked to a stop in front of the partly blocked driveway. The frat boys didn't park so well when they were plastered.

"Thanks." She managed to push the door open and climb out, though it wasn't pretty or graceful. She gave a vague wave as he drove off. She went round to the back door and inserted her key.

There should be a sign over the door, she thought blearily, as she pushed the door open.

Abandon hope all ye who enter here.

2

ZACH BAKER WAS ALREADY SITTING at the battered kitchen table —thirteen kids was a cruel fate for any piece of furniture— reading the news on the tablet the siblings had gone in together to buy for him when the newspaper went digital. He continued to mutter about "changes," but Laura had seen him playing solitaire on it the other day.

Changes indeed.

The room smelled of freshly brewed coffee—torture for someone who couldn't afford to imbibe if she wanted to sleep.

Zach's gaze lifted from his device. "See you made the news."

Laura almost asked him how he'd recognized her butt, but managed to stop herself. She was over thirty, but she still didn't dare sass her dad. Alex claimed you weren't safe from a soap mouth washing until you were at least thirty-five.

"It happens," she admitted. She passed through to her bedroom and took a quick shower, and slipped on sweats and a tee shirt. Her bed beckoned, but when Zach said anything before seven, it meant he was lonely. Or needed to talk about something. None of the Baker clan were what you'd call morning people.

She returned to the kitchen and popped a couple of slices of bread into the toaster. Without the rustle of newspaper pages to break the silence, the toast popping up sounded very loud. She buttered the two slices and then carried them to the table on a plate that she positioned partway between her and her dad. She picked up one and bit in. She was almost too tired to chew, but the butter reminded her taste buds why they existed.

Zach picked up the other piece, another sign he had something to say. Why, she wondered, did the Baker men have such a hard time squeezing words out their mouths? They'd been born with all the necessary parts. If she'd known her dad would get a girlfriend—she winced and changed the thought to—if she'd known Becca would happen, she would have held off moving in. He could have told her not to come home, of course, but it would be easier to negotiate with North Korea than get her dad to tell any of his children they couldn't move home. Becca. Her tired brain kind of froze on the memory of how they'd looked at each other during Alex and Nell's wedding festivities. It was a bit freaky to see your dad looking like that at someone. She'd sort of assumed he was past that, but clearly, he wasn't. The one thing she didn't want, was to come home one morning and run into her dad's girlfriend. She winced again.

She was prepared to be mature, to be happy if her dad was happy. Heaven knows they would have liked him to be happy sooner. But she could see why a man who'd lost two wives and been left with thirteen children would have a hard time finding a date.

They both crunched in silence. Laura realized she'd have to break the conversational ice if she ever wanted to get to bed. But what—she remembered the beads. He'd see through it, but he also might know something about them. He had lived long and seen a lot. She pulled them out, freed them from the paper towel and set them on the table, between them.

"What's this?" he asked, lifting his cheaters up to rest on his head as he picked them up.

"A dying man's last gift," she said. She touched them, making them swing so that they caught the light coming in through the window over the sink. "Because he liked blondes."

Zach's lips twisted in a half grin, half grimace. "Bad?"

"Hit and run."

The grimace won. Zach didn't really approve of her job, even though the family motto was "protect and serve." Girls...well, he was an old-fashioned guy living in a changed world—and too old to adapt himself to fit it.

He fingered the Krewe badge, turning it in the light, then lowering his glasses to study it. "That's an old Krewe." He leaned back thinking. Then shook his head. "I know I've seen it, but don't think it was a New Orleans Krewe. Pretty bauble."

"Very." She brushed the crumbs from her chin, then wiped her hands on her sweatpants. "I almost tossed it."

"Would have been a pity. Might be worth something." He fingered the blue bauble, a frown between his brows. Finally, he shook his head again. "This getting old..."

Laura didn't argue with him or protest that he was only as old as he felt. Maddie, the youngest "baby girl" of the family and a lawyer, always did. But Laura saw old every day, up close and personal. From this side of things, it sucked. Must be worse on his side of things.

She'd give him another minute and then she'd have to hit the sheets before her head hit the tabletop.

"You've met Becca," he muttered, still looking at the beads, so he wouldn't have to look at Laura.

More than once, but... "Yeah," she kept it casual. "She's nice."

"She is. She's...very..." He set the beads down, and his hands started to tap the tabletop. "We went to high school together."

Laura eyed this sign of unease warily. He'd told them how he met Becca at the wedding. And at the reception and a couple of times since. That's pretty much all they knew because Zach and words...

"The thing is, the son of a friend of hers is in town, and, well, you know, three..."

The fact that he was not looking at her, just made it worse. He was as uncomfortable as she was with the idea of a double date. Oh my gosh, if there was anything worse than siblings in love, it was your dad...

"I'm not off until Thursday," she said. His face didn't change, but his shoulders relaxed a bit.

"Thursday is good. I'll find out what time from Becca."

When she was less tired, she was going to cry about this. A blind date *and* a double date with her dad. Oh, the joy.

3

ARCHIBALD GUNN DID NOT like blind dates, but he would take this one, and be grateful, even if fate was rumbling ominously in the background. Fate and luck. Was it good or bad luck? He'd gotten a vague "tip" that he should go to New Orleans, which is why he'd accepted the wedding invitation, even though he hated weddings.

If he hadn't come...

If he hadn't turned on the news...

If he hadn't known someone in the NOPD...

If Becca Poole, his mom's old friend, hadn't called when she had and said what she'd said...

The shock was wearing off. But what was left in its wake wasn't much better.

Anger. The icy kind that came when an old wound was ripped wide open.

Questions. So many questions. Needing answers he wasn't sure he'd get even if—

Don't go there, he told himself. Not yet. He didn't know, not yet. He needed to see it. Touch it. He might not have seen what he thought he'd seen. Even if his punched gut said his eyes had seen exactly what he thought they'd seen. And when he knew? Then? Then stuff would happen, but first, he needed to know.

If a blind date—and a double date with the blind date's dad —was the only way, so be it.

Becca had insisted on picking him up from his hotel, and he found he was glad for it as she steered a complicated path around a Mardi Gras parade route. The need for casual chatting with Becca, the drive through unfamiliar streets, and the distant sound of music from the parade helped to bring him back to a sort of normal. Hopefully, it was enough normal to get him through the evening.

The smells that flooded his senses when he opened the door for Becca reminded him that yes, he had lots of questions, but he was also a human that needed sustenance. And if the food was as good as it smelled...

As he followed Becca to their reserved table, he was forced to admit that his mom had been right. He liked Becca. She was good people. He needed that right now. It was, he conceded to himself, a contradiction to be annoyed about his mom and her friend trying to set him up, and grateful for the "in" it gave him with Laura Baker.

Laura Baker.

In the short time he'd had, there was nothing about her or her family to raise any flags or provide a link—he cut that thought off. Too soon to go there. It was interesting that in a city that had always struggled with corruption, no one had anything bad to say about any of the Bakers, at least not in the context of doing anything illegal. There were a lot of them, they were good at what they did, and some of them had ruffled some feathers in the process. His source had sighed some about how good-looking the daughters were and how hard they were to access through the brother screen.

"I was afraid you'd be annoyed with us." Becca's voice broke into his thoughts as he helped her get seated.

"Annoyed?" Had he missed something?

"About the blind date?" she prodded gently, real concern in her eyes.

"It's dinner," he pointed out.

Becca's smile had beamed out, startling him. That's why the old boy was so interested. "You're right, but it's also..." she hesitated, then added almost thoughtfully, "an act of trust."

Gunn blinked. Trust? Had she guessed—

"When one person cares about a friend and then introduces them to another friend, isn't that about trust?"

"I've never thought about it that way," Gunn admitted. But then, this was the first time he'd been set up by an old friend of his mother's and not a buddy who was trying to even out a third-wheel situation. If he'd been standing, he might have shuffled his feet in guilt. Becca's trust was in Gunn's mom, not him. Why he was here tonight, why he'd said yes—the last person he could tell was his mom.

"You like Laura?" he probed. He couldn't afford guilt right now.

"She's been very kind to me, not that any of them have been unkind," she hastened to add. "They've been very...grown up."

Gunn considered this statement before nodding slowly. "We don't always feel grown up about our parents."

He was rewarded with another of Becca's smiles. It carried him back, way back, to his first teacher and his first gold star. His teacher's smile had been nicer than any gold star. He might have had his first crush on her. This thought brought the guilt back, but lucky for him Becca straightened, her gaze moving past him. He glanced at his watch. Bang on time. He half turned in his seat and got his first, real-time look at Laura Baker.

He wasn't sure if it was the woman, because his mom had

taught him to rise for women, or both manners and Laura, but he found himself standing as she approached. Not that he cared why because his eyes liked what they saw. He'd expected just okay, despite his source's assessment, he realized because she hadn't looked this good on the TV. Of course, on TV she'd been covered in muck and blood.

She wasn't now.

Tall with her blonde hair swinging free against her shoulders—it had been confined on TV—she moved like fast, fresh water. One thing hadn't changed between TV and now. Her chin had a lot of determination in its clean, crisp lines. As she wove between the tables, her dress clinging in all the right places, he felt almost tense as he waited for her to notice him.

Her gaze, above a coolly polite smile, was still scanning the room. After a quick glance at her old man, he kept his gaze on hers waiting to see her first reaction to him, telling himself that his tense anticipation was about answers and not because she was easy on the eyes—

Her old man shifted to block his view, his hard gaze a pointed reminder that this fishing expedition had a few obstacles. Gunn hastily reined in his appreciation. The old man looked like he'd seen all the looks a guy could have, knew what they meant, and didn't like any of them directed at his little girl. Gunn met the old man's gaze without flinching, but it wasn't easy. And then Zach Baker's gaze narrowed sharply. Baker might be retired, but he still had a cop's instincts.

That was gonna increase the level of difficulty a bit.

When her dad's gaze finally shifted to *his* girlfriend, Gunn drew in a relieved breath.

Baker reached the table and bent down to kiss Becca on the cheek. Gunn noticed that Laura managed to not see the exchange of greetings as she moved around the table. He pulled out the chair next to his for Laura, knowing his smile was friendlier than he'd planned, as Becca performed the introductions. Being a friend of hers didn't help with the dad as much as he'd hoped, though his hand closing around Laura's removed some of the sting. He liked the soft feel of her skin against his and the directness in her blue-gray eyes. Her features were clean, both her jaw and the polite curve of her mouth still managed to show signs of the determination he'd witnessed during her approach. He'd have to be careful. He'd bet real money that pretty nose could smell a rat—in or out of a New Orleans alley.

As they settled in their seats, the food smells in the air were briefly broken by something sweet and flowery—from her he presumed. It suited her.

The waiter appeared and took drink orders. Mineral water with a slice of lime was Laura's order. Zach and Becca didn't order alcohol either. Gunn ordered a soft drink then opened his menu and gave Laura a smile across the top.

"What do you recommend?" he asked.

———

This was probably the best blind date she'd ever had, though the blind date bar was super low. Laura didn't let her imagination—or her heart—run away with her. In her experience, guys could be charming and lots of other adjectives and then walk away, never to be heard from again.

Would she mind?

She scooped the last bite of rice into her mouth and chewed thoughtfully, careful not to look at Archie while she did.

He hadn't made a good impression on Zach, but she'd yet to meet the man who could get past her dad's "that's my little girl" prejudices. Never mind she was over thirty and had been living on her own until her apartment got turned into condos, and she got guilted by her many siblings into moving back home to "take care of dad."

She needed to find a way to get back at them, she reminded herself. And, if she was reading the signs right, she needed to speed up her hunt for a new place now that they'd upped the game with the blind/double date.

Not that she had a lot to complain about, but there was a principle here, a line that had been crossed that must not ever be crossed again.

She slanted a peek at Archie. He wasn't super good-looking or socially inept. His movements were confident, and his shoulders were broad enough to indicate reliability when one factored in the steadiness of his brown-eyed gaze. His mouth was on the stern side, but it had several times softened into a charm-laden smile that might have encouraged her toes to curl a teensy bit. His brown hair was lightly dusted with both white and gray. He wasn't loud or assertive, but managed to hold his own against Zach's, well, it could only be called an interrogation.

Both Laura and Becca gave him apologetic looks when Zach paused to contemplate his food. They were rewarded with a quirk of his lips that hinted at a sense of humor. And, she realized, he managed to give the impression of answering Zach's questions without actually telling them that much about himself.

Zach hadn't realized that. That would come later. But for now, her dad had relaxed enough to let them all eat and chat— mostly about New Orleans, which was typical. Archie managed to eat and indicate enjoyment in said food without getting all weird about it. Her last blind date had practically had a Meg Ryan food-gasm. This had resulted in her pulling all blind date privileges from all her brothers. If any of them had produced a guy like Archie...

Her gaze met Becca's across the table and Laura found it

much easier to smile at her. If nothing else came of this night, she knew she could trust Becca to not set her up with a jerk. It also helped Laura not stiffen when Becca brought up Laura's moment of "glory" on television.

"I couldn't believe it when I recognized you," Becca said. "I don't think I've ever personally known someone who was on TV." The glint of humor in Becca's eyes prompted Laura's mouth to turn up at the edges. She ignored Zach's sudden scowl.

"Considering what I was covered with, I was hoping no one would recognize me." She gave a soft chuckle. "I think almost everyone I know saw me. I mean, what are the odds of that?"

"Do I dare admit I saw you, too?" Archie said.

Laura half covered her face with one hand. "Good thing you didn't know who your blind date was with tonight. I have showered several times since then."

This sent a chuckle around the table, though Laura expected Zach to tweak her later about mentioning that she showered in front of a guy. In an odd twist, she half sensed that Archie's chuckle was a bit off. Did he wish he wasn't with her now that he knew? Or was she being hypersensitive? Probably the latter. Women, she well knew, tended to over analyze everything. And with five sisters, it was more like über over analyzing.

"What was the filthy thing hanging down your back?" Becca wanted to know. "It was like no piece of medical equipment I've ever seen."

Laura laughed, aware that hers now felt ever so slightly off as the events of that night came back to her. The damp chill of the January air. The look in the guy's eyes as blood bubbled out his mouth—

"The victim gave her some Mardi Gras beads," Zach said.

It was a relief to have her dad's voice slice through her thoughts, but it also made her blink in surprise. Perhaps it was

Becca who had prompted this unusual animation in his face and voice. Was this what Zach was like as Zach and not as Dad?

"They looked old, like they used to make them back in the day. With glass," he added.

Laura's eyes widened some more as Zach began to share a little of the history of Mardi Gras beads. She wished she could film this because none of the sibs would believe it. With Zach focused on Becca, the only person left to share her shock with was Archie, but he was staring at Zach with a sharply narrowed, strangely intent gaze.

"I suppose even glass beads are somewhat valuable if they are old," Becca said thoughtfully.

Zach shifted so that he leaned a bit more in Becca's direction. "I asked a friend of mine to check them out."

He had? Laura felt her eyebrows arch but bit back an instinctive protest she couldn't explain to herself, let alone her dad. She glanced at Archie again and saw tension digging deep lines on either side of his mouth. Suddenly it didn't feel like she was over-thinking anything. As if he sensed her gaze, his chest—his very nice chest—rose and fell in a sigh and he looked at her, his expression easing into polite inquiry mixed with concern. One of his brows arched in a question. Since she didn't know the question, she was left to wonder how he'd made just one brow arch. Hers only rose or fell together.

He sipped some of his soft drink. "It was a hit and run, wasn't it?" His low toned inquiry couldn't have been heard across the table where Zach was still expounding all things Mardi Gras bead.

She nodded, the tension shifting to her face now. She'd learned to let go after her shift, to not take her work home with her, but that had somehow changed when she brought the beads home.

"Tough job," he said.

His tone hadn't changed, but Laura sensed he knew how tough. Her mind went back over Zach's interrogation, and she realized at no point had Archie told them what he did.

She nodded again, trying to decide how to ask, but before she could, Archie pushed back his plate and sighed.

"That was some seriously good food."

"Zach knows where all the good food is buried." Laura grinned at her dad.

"Don't have to pay fancy prices to find good food." Zach's lips might have twitched. Then his eyes and mouth lost their humor. Round two of the interrogation of Archie Gunn was about to commence.

Laura wanted to know, but not because her dad asked, so she put in before he could speak, "Anyone else want dessert?"

Possibly not a good dating decision to have dessert on top of her platter of shrimp and sides, but the date was a double with her *dad*. Even if the blind date was her preferred type of hot, all she was getting tonight was grilled by her dad when she got home. So she was getting dessert. And she was eating all of it.

"Absolutely," Becca said, her gaze sympathetic.

If she could get Zach to chill, Laura would join Team Becca as a cheerleader.

"I'm in," Archie said, his smile making a brief, but heart stuttering, appearance.

As her answering smile flashed out, she felt her dad try to kill her buzz with a look. Since this whole blind date thing was his fault, she ignored the stare, keeping her attention on Archie, maybe even boosting her smile because it would annoy her dad and right now he couldn't do anything about it. Archie looked so...well, so un-sinister that she started to wonder if she was paranoid. There was no question her dating life sucked, so paranoid was an easy place to go. Her dad didn't want her to date at all and her brothers, well, they didn't mind if she dated wimps.

Anyone they liked? Not gonna happen. They were guys, and they knew what guys like them were thinking. There was something rather hilarious about the fact that it was Zach who had set her up with someone her brothers would like her to never date.

"What do you recommend?" Archie added, also keeping his gaze directed away from Zach. He leaned in so they could share the dessert menu, their shoulders brushing together in a distinctly friendly way.

"Bread pudding," Laura and Becca said at the same time.

"Bread pudding it is," Archie said.

Laura and Becca looked at Zach. Laura tried to keep her expression bland as her dad twisted on the horns of his own dilemma. He loved bread pudding, but he did have his pride. Finally, he sighed.

"Bread pudding."

It did taste better than pride.

4

THEY SEPARATED at the curb outside, Zach being steered gently, but firmly away by Becca. Laura had her car back from Frank and had offered Archie a ride to his hotel before Zach could. It wasn't a desire to navigate New Orleans streets during Mardi Gras season as much as it was an assertion of her independence, though thankfully most of the traffic, party and otherwise, had died down.

It was humid, but cool enough it wasn't unpleasant. According to the news, there was a cold front coming. Or maybe it had already arrived. The word cold covered a range of temperatures from actual cold to "not as hot."

There were shadows outside the light caused by the storefronts and streetlights, but they weren't deep unless one wandered where one shouldn't. Laura felt Archie's gaze on her while they waited for the valet to bring her car around. She expected him to comment on her dad, but he surprised her.

"Do your victims give you gifts often?" he asked.

She shook her head. "That was a first for me." She hesitated. "We have had accident victims send thank you notes and sometimes flowers to our station. They might bond a little and want to thank us in person, but life goes on." Her lips twitched as more memories stirred. "One guy told me he'd made a promise to God that if he survived he'd find me and propose."

"He must have lived."

"And was relieved when I turned him down." She gave a soft laugh.

"Were you a little tempted?"

The humor that softened his mouth? That was tempting. "The poor man had survived a car crash. It would have been inhumane to ask him to survive my brothers."

"And your dad," Archie added.

"And my dad," Laura agreed. She slanted him a sideways look, aware her eyes liked what they saw. Could she trust senses that told her different things about him? Or was it the good food and good looks that wanted to weigh in on him being a good guy? "Sorry about my dad, by the way. He used to be a cop, so interrogating people comes naturally to him."

"Not a problem," Archie said easily.

He stood relaxed, his feet apart and planted, his thumbs hooked in the front pockets of his jeans. Okay, his well-fitting jeans. His jacket hung comfortably loose from the shoulders she'd admired earlier. If it weren't so quiet, she'd have sighed. Maybe it was hanging with Zach and Becca. Was romance catching? She usually stayed too busy to worry about her lack of a love life, but tonight, with some soft jazz drifting in on the breeze and Archie's distinctly male cologne filling her nostrils, she'd wished for her dad not to have been the one sitting across the table from her.

She realized that Archie was looking at her and might have flushed a little, giving thanks for the poor light. All at once aware of how alone they were, her earlier doubts trickled back in, not in a flood. She was too tired, too full and too—something for that.

"You parried very well," she said, wishing his face wasn't quite so shadowed. He didn't stiffen or anything dramatic, but she sensed a return of tension from him.

He cast her a glance that was almost wary. "I might have had some practice with fathers."

She processed this for a few seconds. "You've been married." It wasn't a question and it was a question. If he was still married, then it was also a problem.

"Divorced," he admitted. He paused. "Twice."

"I'm glad Zach didn't ferret that out." She was pleased with how calm she sounded. It was something to process later—and there was something in his tone that was a definite warning flag to going in any deeper with him. He'd done it twice and was done, she sensed. It was a pity, she admitted. What she knew about him so far, she liked. She shoved her hands into the pockets of her pants and stared down the street. A car was heading slowly toward them. Was her car finally here?

"Dads are dads," Archie said, his voice neutral.

"All the world over," she agreed. Not her car, she realized. The headlights weren't right. It seemed to be accelerating, but then light hit from the other direction as another car turned the corner. Her car—no, this was a patrol car. It pulled into the curb, even though it was the wrong direction. The window lowered, and the cop who'd tried to chat her up at the hit and run poked his head out. His gaze moved from her to Archie, then back to her as the other car swung wide to pass the NOPD vehicle.

"You all right, ma'am?" he asked.

Ma'am. So maybe she'd been wrong about him hitting on her.

"Just waiting for our car," she assured him. She glanced at Archie, but he was watching the other car disappear down the street, his expression bland, but somehow dangerous, too.

———

Archie settled into the passenger side of Laura's car as well as he could. Apparently, she was not as long as she'd looked, because she tucked in easily.

"You can push the seat back a little more, I think," Laura said. "It's on the side."

Her attention was on her mirrors as she pulled out onto the quiet street. For a few seconds, her car's headlights lit up a car pulled to the side of the street in the next block, picking out the silhouettes of two people inside. It looked a lot like the one that had passed them when the cop had stopped. Maybe he was paranoid, but it seemed like an odd—not to mention dangerous—place to be sitting in a car. This section of the street was all warehouse fronts locked down for the night.

They'd traveled another city block before headlights appeared behind them. He settled back, taking another look in the side mirror. No way to tell if it was the same car that had pulled in behind them or a random car that had turned onto the street, so he might as well look at Laura, who was easier on the eyes than a streetlight-washed road.

Her gaze was on the road ahead, her grip on the steering wheel just the right amount of relaxed, the scent of a woman's perfume, and good food lingering in the air despite the current of air coming out the vents. The lowered light was kind, but she didn't need kind and if her bone structure were any indication, wouldn't ever need soft lighting to look good. He liked the way her blonde hair moved against the skin covering her good bones. Liked her profile and the slight purse of her lips, it was safe—for now—to contemplate tasting. He knew she was smart, that she worked hard, and liked her food. If he could have afforded to get distracted, this was the woman he'd pick.

The essential question wasn't "did he want to kiss her,"

because who wouldn't? Archie checked the side mirror again. The headlights had closed a bit. No, his main worry right now was, were they being followed? And if they were, had he drawn danger to her or had she brought it by being on the news?

He considered the woman next to him. As if she sensed his scrutiny, she stopped for a light and looked at him.

"It can't be my driving."

"What?"

"That's making you tense," she pointed out, sending the car forward again as the light changed to green.

"Sorry." He couldn't stop his gaze straying to the side mirror once more. The headlights started to close in on them. A car pulled out in front of them, then began to slow. A frown formed between her neat brows and he felt her go on alert, even as he opened his mouth to warn her...

He and his words went sideways as she made a sharp left down an alley. She sent the car forward nicely, maintained control as she wove through the common alley obstacles. She braked again, then made a calm left back onto a city street. About halfway down this street, she made a sudden u-turn. The tires protested a bit, but they ended up parked neatly almost in front of a police station. A cop, who had been walking up the steps, paused and looked around, then came down to the driver's side of the car. He leaned an arm on the hood as Laura rolled down the window.

"Laura. I thought I recognized your car, *chère*." His smile was easy, friendly like someone who'd known her a long time. His gaze lifted as a car passed on the other side. His smile didn't change, but his gaze was alert. He bent again, this time giving Archie the once over. "Problem?"

"I noticed the time and wondered if Cal needed a ride home."

Cal. Calvin was one of the brothers, Archie recalled.

A long silence as the cop processed this. Then he gave a slow nod.

"You just missed him." The cop's gaze strayed to Archie again.

Archie met the gaze blandly, ignoring the question in them.

"Don't think I've seen you around?" the cop persisted.

"This is Archie, George. Archie, this is George. Archie's a friend of Becca's," Laura added.

"Becca. That's Zach's new..." Laura's gaze turned toward him, and George coughed. "...friend. Met her at Alex's wedding."

"She's very nice," Laura said as if he'd asked. "Well, thanks, George. See you around."

"I'll tell Cal you stopped by," George said, stepping back from the car.

He lifted an arm in a last wave. They drove in silence, this time making it to his hotel without interruption or signs of being followed. Laura pulled into a spot that was not front and center or in the shadow and turned off the ignition. Then she angled to face him. Her gaze considered him for long enough that it took some willpower for him not to shift in his seat.

"Can I buy you a cup of coffee?" Archie finally asked. She was pretty in a way her dad wasn't, but the gaze right now was very like the old man's.

She let the silence build some more, then removed the key from the ignition and opened her door. "It will have to be decaf," she said.

———

Laura could feel Archie thinking as he followed her inside. He didn't try to steer her toward the elevator—which was smart. Instead, he followed her into the relatively quiet lounge just off the main lobby. This was New Orleans at night. Total quiet wouldn't happen until closer to morning.

Once inside the lounge, Archie took over, herding her toward a corner with no one on either side and a view of the door. He left her alone while he collected two coffees on a tray with creamer and sugar options, then settled in next to her, close enough so they could hear each other, but enough distance so he could watch her face.

Normally, she didn't think this much about a blind date. Of course, normally she would already be home. Her dad was not above texting her when she missed the curfew that should have ended when she turned eighteen. His house, his rules. Most nights she didn't mind playing the dad card, but tonight she was curious. So she mixed real sugar and real cream into her decaf, all the while watching Archie through the veil of her lashes.

Earlier, she'd been embarrassed to find out he'd seen her on the news, but now it was part of the growing puzzle that was Archie Gunn. As the almost youngest of the siblings, Laura had had ample opportunity to devise a wide variety of coping skills, which included a poker face she'd been told was almost world-class. It certainly helped with her job that she could, in the heat of the moment, detach her emotions and focus on what needed to be done. Her observation skills were also highly developed. With that many siblings ahead of her, it paid to stay alert.

"I thought I was going to have to apologize," she said, lifting her lashes and spearing him with a gaze she knew—from long experience—had a good chance of catching Archie off guard. He hid it better than most, but his lashes flickered, and for a couple of seconds confusion showed in his dark eyes.

"Apologize?" His lips quirked at the edges.

"For my brothers." His brows arched, so she added. "I thought one of them was tailing us."

"Is that something they do a lot?" He didn't try to hide his amusement now.

"More than you'd think they'd have time for." She hesitated. "But it wasn't a brother."

"You're sure?"

Yeah, he was trying to deflect her while he thought some more.

"If it had been any of my brothers, they'd have stopped, too. They'd never pass up the chance to grill my date."

"Even if your dad—?"

She shook her head, lifting her cup and sipping to hold back the grin his invited her to reciprocate. The man was loaded with charm. Did he know it? He did, she decided, but not in the annoying way some men had. Some guys could hardly contain their coolness. Others, like Archie, were just quietly confident. Late nights with the sisters, they'd discussed the subject a lot, trying to figure out why one annoyed so much, and the other, well, it didn't. Okay, it didn't annoy all the time.

Archie didn't just have that confidence, Laura had a feeling he could stand up to her brothers, as well, but she was pretty sure that wasn't his plan. And yes, she was now confident that their date hadn't been a date, but a fishing expedition.

A pity. A good thing that the other trait she'd developed as the number twelve kid was pragmatism. It was what it was.

It was nice to know that her instincts were on target and not overthinking or paranoia.

So what was he fishing for?

He'd seen her on TV and what? In her bulky uniform and covered in genuinely awful stuff, she was betting it wasn't about her. So what was it about? She'd been on the screen for maybe thirty seconds. Probably less than that. He hadn't brought it up or questioned her, other than confirming it was a hit and run. Her mind ran over the conversation and came up empty for excessive curiosity. The only thing she recalled was that he got a bit tense when Becca was talking about the Mardi Gras beads, but that could have been her.

Well, they could sit here for what was left of the night not talking. At the moment, it felt a lot like a conversation with her dad, but Archie surprised her by being the first to break the silence.

"The beads," he said, making a movement with his hands as if he were wearing them. "It's hard to know, of course, but they looked like a strand that went," the break was small, "missing some years back."

She considered asking him to clarify "missing" but had a feeling that was all she was going to get tonight.

"So you want to see the strand? You could have, you know, asked," she pointed out.

"I could have," he admitted.

He hadn't trusted them. Okay. She couldn't blame him. He didn't know them. And she didn't know him, she reminded herself. That thought caused a small jolt, a tremor across her nervous system because part of her felt like she did know this man. Okay, that wasn't good. She could not afford to start filling in the gaps, painting a romance where there wasn't one.

Finally, he rubbed his face with both hands. "I wonder if I'm crazy," he admitted.

"It was covered in mud," she said.

"It's the shape of the Krewe badge and the—" his hands moved as if to help his mouth find the word.

"Bauble?" Tiredness started to tug at the edges of her brain and her eyes. Maybe she should have kept the caff in her coffee. Disconnected pieces of the evening floated past. "The tail," she said abruptly. "You think that's why...?"

He leaned back, this time rubbing his forehead with one hand. "Others must have seen the news."

"But—" She frowned as refutations warred with what had happened—what *might* have happened tonight. "There's been no sign that anyone is interested—"

At that moment, her phone started to ping as multiple texts hit. She pulled it out. Didn't have to unlock it to see the problem or that there were multiple texts from multiple siblings. She looked at Archie.

"Someone broke into the house."

"Let's go," Archie said, sliding out from behind the table and holding out his hand.

She looked at him for a second, sighed and took his hand, letting him help her get upright as her phone continued to ping. Was it an official "baking" if the house being baked was the Baker homestead?

5

BAKED.

Laura had tried to warn him. Now he knew what the word meant.

Multiple Baker children were milling inside and outside of the house. He had known there were thirteen of them, but he hadn't realized what that meant in actual human volume until he saw them together, some with significant others in tow. They didn't need a neighborhood crowd to gather — even though one did — when they had each other. They even brought their own flashing red lights. Of course, not all the flashing red were from Bakers. He noticed a few non-Baker cops hanging around, including the one called George they had seen earlier. Archie couldn't tell if George noticed him or not.

Laura introduced him to all her siblings and some of the extras. They probably remembered his name, since he was one person. It was possible he'd sort out their names and faces. Or not. It wasn't need-to-remember. He leaned against a counter, pushed into a corner by the sheer mass of them, hoping he wouldn't ever need to remember. His gaze found Laura in the shifting mass and his hope was tempered some. Something about her, he admitted reluctantly, drew him and it wasn't just the beads.

With all the sisters together, it upped the 'it' factor of them by quite a bit. They were all blonde, all built the way he liked—with enough padding in the right places, so you knew they were female—intelligent and high spirited, so that feminine tones mingled with the male tones almost equally. Individually they were beautiful women, but together, it wasn't unreasonable to consider them stunning. And yet it was Laura who drew his gaze. Not good.

In their midst, like an island, Zach sat at the end of a beat-up kitchen table reading the news on an iPad. Though Laura was in the midst of her sisters, Archie noticed she wasn't contributing a lot to the commentary. Like him, she appeared to be waiting them out. To his relief, she didn't mention his interest in the beads. He liked the quiet way she occupied her space, a small, alert yet somehow peaceful pool of calm, in the midst of chaos.

Slowly, like a plugged drain, the Baker siblings began to leave. From what he could gather, nothing appeared to be missing. Zach had interrupted the ransacking before it reached the kitchen. This did not mean the beads were still here, and he planned not to move until he found out. Interesting that Zach didn't mention them either. He'd risen to give and receive awkward hugs from his sons, warm ones with cheek kisses from his daughters.

In the end, all that remained were he, Laura, and Zach.

When Zach's gaze settled on him, Archie found a good reason to miss the crowd.

"Grab a chair, Archie," Laura said, pulling out one next to her dad. She leaned her elbows on the table, resting her chin in the palm of one hand. Now Archie could see tired blurring the edges of her eyes and mouth. "So, you said you asked a friend about the beads from my hit and run?"

Zach nodded, his wary gaze moving between them, before settling back on Archie. Man, he was glad he wasn't on the other side of the interrogation table from this guy.

He gave a slow nod. "They weren't stolen this evening," Zach said.

Laura rubbed her eyes. "So where are they?"

"I took them to the friend." His gaze flicked toward Archie again. "Had a feeling they were..."

"Valuable?" Laura didn't wait for his response. "They might be. What friend?"

"Henri," Zach released the name reluctantly, giving Archie the impression this friend was of the dubious variety, a not uncommon occurrence for a cop, though why he'd trust him was a whole other question.

Laura looked like she was going to add something, but instead looked at Archie with her brows lifted. He hadn't told her enough to go on with.

"I have an interest in their...provenance," Archie admitted. Zach wasn't the only one in the room who had trouble sharing.

"Do you now." It wasn't really a question.

"Does anyone else know where you took them, Zach?" Laura pressed.

"If that's what they were looking for, I'd say no," Zach said.

"Jeez, Zach, do you have to be such a sphinx?"

Zach's gaze shot to her, turning über-dad on her.

"Sorry, but—" She stopped and bit her lip. She finally shook her head and leaned back in the chair. "It's too late for dancing. Why Henri?"

Zach's expression may have softened some. Or it was the light. "Henri is something of an expert on vintage beads. He was going to call me in the morning, but I'll admit he seemed a mite surprised when he saw them."

Laura glanced at Archie, once more handing him the conversational ball.

"Because they were a copy?" Archie asked.

Zach rubbed his chin before responding. "What he said to me was that they *should* be a copy."

"But..." This from Laura.

"If they were a copy, they were the best copy he'd ever seen," Zach admitted.

———

The night had been too short, mostly because it had passed during the hours of the morning without her actually sleeping that much. Laura, like most of her siblings, was not a morning person. And yet here, though she was not sure how, she was at the butt crack of dawn with Zach and Archie, driving to Henri's through almost silent streets.

Archie, she noticed, was back on 'are we being tailed' alert. No surprise Zach had noticed that. At least her dad hadn't grilled her before or during breakfast. She figured he was saving that for lunch. After they cut Archie loose. She glanced at Archie.

He would not be that easy to cut loose unless he wanted to be released back into the wild. Did he? Once they were all in the same room as the beads, what happened then? Technically, they belonged to her until their provenance — fancy word that — was worked out. Archie seemed to think he'd know when he saw them.

But, for argument's sake, assuming they were the same, then what? Why did these beads matter so much? Because they did matter. He might look relaxed, but he was a coiled spring of tension.

Before she'd finally fallen asleep last—this morning—she'd

gone over and over in her mind her interaction with the victim. It hadn't taken long. She'd made assumptions about him, based on the location the car had tossed him and the thickness of the muck coating his body when she should have paid more attention to his warning. Were the beads "treasure?"

"We should check with Hannah—" she broke the silence suddenly— "see if anyone claimed the body."

Neither man asked for further elucidation. She might be a little impressed that Archie hadn't asked who Hannah was, but perhaps he'd checked out her family and already knew? Not to mention, had figured out what body she referred to.

She felt the urge, or perhaps it was the longing, to be in two places at once. They needed to get their hands on the beads, but it could only reveal one fact. If they were real or not.

It was unlikely there'd been an autopsy on her hit and run. The cause of death was apparent, and the coroner's office was always behind. No one said it out loud, but there tended to be a political calculation in whether an autopsy happened. If no one had claimed the body, then there might be clues or something in his personal belongings. If. That was not a given either, she suspected.

Who he was, where he'd been, those were things they might learn if they looked. Unless Archie had already followed that fox? It had been two days since the hit and run. Had Archie already connected the dots between her and the victim or orchestrated the "blind" date, or had that been all luck? Did she want to know if Archie would have said no to the date without the necklace in play?

Probably not, she decided. And he'd checked her out. She could see this in hindsight. Mostly, her dates exhibited shock and awe when they found out how many siblings she had. Archie had been amused. He had not been shocked.

So, what did he do that gave him access to checking people

out? He still hadn't shared his line of work with them. She'd assumed law enforcement because he gave off the same vibes as Zach and her brothers. But he'd never said.

Without sharing why, Laura pulled out her cell and speed dialed Hannah. She was pretty sure she was working today. She put it on speaker because that would be simpler than explaining.

"Hey." Hannah's voice was somewhat distracted as if she were up to her elbows in a body.

"Do you remember the hit and run that got me on the news the other day?"

"Well, I remember you being on the news."

"Could you find out who logged in the body and if it's still there? Also any personal items."

There was a long pause.

"Did you change your job without telling anyone?" Hannah asked.

"Just do as she asks," Zach put in with an extra level of terse.

Another longer silence.

"Sure thing. Um, as soon as I stitch this guy up."

"Thanks," Laura said. "Love you."

"Love you, too." Maybe it was the connection that made her sound so ironic as she ended the call.

"Thanks," Archie said.

"Take a right into that alley coming up," Zach directed.

Archie took the turn, easing her car down the narrow lane past a shabby mix of single and two-story shotgun houses. He didn't need to be told it was the one with the rear door hanging ominously open. He braked hard, then flung his door open.

"Call it in," Zach ordered as he ran after Archie.

Laura yanked out her phone again, feeling a highly inappropriate longing to video her dad running. Instead, she stabbed in nine-one-one. So much irony.

6

Archie found Henri, at least he figured it was Henri, lying face-down under a pile of debris that looked like it had been thrown from the shelves that lined both sides of the narrow passageway. Faded linoleum was randomly visible between scattered heaps of watches, necklaces, rings, and other small items of adornment. Papers from a desk with the drawers hanging open added to the impression that a frenzied search had been conducted around the fallen man.

Archie pushed some of the debris off him and had his finger on Henri's pulse when Zach came in. His gaze flicked up to meet the older man, who leaned against the rifled desk, trying not to look like he was catching his breath.

"Not dead." He paused. "Yet." His gaze went past Zach to Laura who gave a cautious look inside, then ran forward, pushed aside the debris on the other side of Henri, and dropped to her knees.

"Call for an ambulance, Zach," she said, her tone decidedly un-daughter-like. She dug inside her purse and extracted a pair of surgical gloves. Perhaps she saw or felt his surprise. "Never go anywhere without them."

She started a careful check of his injuries, while a still-winded Zach called for an ambulance. The sirens that began to wail in the background would be police from Laura's call, Archie guessed.

Henri stirred and moaned.

"Try not to move," Laura said gently. "An ambulance is on the way."

"Ogre..." he muttered.

Archie looked at Zach, his brow arched.

"My hit and run said the same thing," Laura admitted, with a wary look at Archie.

Zach, not without some difficulty, crouched by Henri's head.

"Henri, it's Zach. Did they get the necklace? The beads? Did they find them?"

His head moved in a feeble negative. Laura looked annoyed at the questions but didn't stop them.

"Where is it?"

"Saw...coming...hid..." His voice trailed off.

"No more," Laura said, her attention on Henri. A second wail joined the first, which could be heard coming up the alley.

Archie rose and jerked his chin. With obvious reluctance, Zach rose and followed Archie into the shambles of the front room. More papers had been tossed from yanked open drawers. A wide variety of merchandise—with dubious provenance Archie didn't doubt—had been flung from even more dusty and rickety shelves on one side of what was probably supposed to be a living room. The debris—and the fact that Henri was on the bottom of it—supported his contention he'd seen trouble coming. That he'd hidden the necklace did not mean they hadn't found it. And how had Henri known that's what they were after?

"How can he be sure they didn't find it?"

"As someone who has executed the occasional search

warrant here, I'm going with they didn't find it." Zach sounded rueful and a bit defensive.

Why had he given the necklace to this guy?

Henri stirred again, as footsteps could be heard approaching from the alley.

Archie grabbed a chair, pushed a pile of stuff aside and set it near Henri's head, gesturing for Zach to sit. Zach did, though he glared at Archie first.

"Henri, who did you call?" Zach asked.

"Not...ogre...never ogre..."

Zach frowned, and half shook his head. "Then who?"

"Not ba...by..."

Before Archie could ask, their backup arrived, and on their heels were a couple of EMS techs.

———

Laura got out of the way for the on-duty EMS techs with equipment. She gave them a quick summary of what she'd found on arrival, then backed off. The two patrol cops—not relatives, thank goodness—were questioning Zach and Archie near the broken rear door, but she had a feeling the scene was gonna get baked sooner rather than later. If she remembered right, Alex was on duty today. And Ingrid? She'd just started back to work after getting shot a couple of months ago, but on "light" duty— weekends only—which meant, if she wasn't already on scene somewhere she could be showing up soon. And if word got out that Zach was here?

Oh yeah, baking would commence.

Laura looked around. The search looked like it had been fast and dirty. Had it stopped because they found what they were looking for or because they were interrupted? Just because Henri believed they hadn't found the beads didn't make it so.

And why were they all so sure this was about the beads? It was clear that Henri was not an upstanding citizen. So why had Zach given him the beads?

One of the techs looked up. "Knife wound," he said briefly.

She nodded and moved casually away, taking care not to touch anything, but also getting out of sight of the cops. She wasn't going to search, but there was no law against looking.

The scent of old, sad coffee, sweat, and stale beer lingered in the air. Bacon, too, she decided and was unsurprised when she found a half-eaten breakfast of eggs and bacon on the table with some tumbled beer empties scattered across the top. A chair was shoved back. It appeared that the search had ended about halfway through this room. The front door was slightly ajar. She glanced back, then eyed the stairs. She was tempted, but logic said they'd have caught him coming down the stairs if he'd run up there to stash the beads. Unless they'd searched there first...

She hesitated and then it was too late. The front door was pushed wider, and her brother Alex's broad shoulders blocked most of the light. The crime scene baking had begun. Ferris caught sight of her in a gap not blocked by Alex. His eyes widened, and then he gave her a sympathetic look.

Alex's scowl was going to get worse, so Laura deployed her big brother glare shield and then tossed him a distracting bone.

"Zach's here," she said and watched with satisfaction as his attention shifted past her. He didn't push her aside because she knew to get out of his way. Did she know how to deflect or did she know how to deflect? A pity none of the sisters were here to share a fist bump with her.

Ferris pulled out his notebook and stepped to the side, glancing back as the CSU truck pulled up behind their car. No surprise a small crowd had started to gather. If it got big enough the Lucky Dog truck would show up, and they'd all get some lunch.

She saw her sister Ingrid climbing down. She'd never done a crime scene with Ingrid so this would be interesting.

"I figure you'd rather I took your statement," Ferris said, giving Alex's back a quick look before he deployed a grin.

Laura's nod might have been a tad emphatic. "Will this take long? I need to meet up with Hannah."

Distracting Ferris was almost as easy as distracting Alex. No question Ferris' gaze softened. The guy had it bad for Laura's big sister. His gaze tracked past Laura again, his attention on the fallen Henri.

"We were hoping she'd get off early today."

"Sorry." She saw Ferris' face change into a half frown and looked back in time to see Archie approaching. Past Henri, Alex loomed over Zach, something that still didn't give her brother an advantage over their dad. Zach's flat dad stare cut Alex down to size. He wasn't shuffling his feet yet, but he was close. She'd have thought Zach's oldest—and thus the one who had lived the longest with Zach—would have learned not to go at their dad breathing fire and outrage. Zach had the bigger firehose.

"Your dad is the bomb," Ferris said with a grin, but his curious gaze shifted back to Archie.

"A bomb that goes off with some regularity," Laura pointed out. Archie reached her side, changing the dynamics even as she performed introductions. "Archie Gunn. Logan Ferris, my brother Alex's partner. Archie is a friend of Becca's, Logan," she added with more than a smidge of guilty mischief.

"Not the—" Logan stopped before he said "girlfriend," but it didn't matter. His look of dismay said it all.

Zach was challenging enough without his girlfriend swirled into the mix. There. She'd thought "girlfriend" without flinching. Progress.

The two men shook hands like a couple of warily circling

dudes trying to figure out if they were gonna be friends or foes. She might have sighed at the sudden rise of testosterone.

"What brings you here? No one died," Laura pointed out.

"Henri's address always gets our attention," Ferris explained, then his gaze shifted from friend to detective. "What brings you here?"

She hesitated and then fell back on the tried and true. "It wasn't me."

The two men exchanged looks.

"Well, it wasn't."

Archie earned a few brownie points by half nodding, half shrugging.

Logan looked past her with a "please, say it isn't so" look erasing the detective one. "Your dad?"

"Sorry," Laura said, even though she really wasn't.

———

Archie had to give Laura a lot of credit for taking the spotlight off them and putting it on her old man. He'd have been suspicious of her deflecting skills, but the lady had twelve siblings—a number it was not easy to wrap his brain around. In fact, he'd thought his deflecting skills were of a pretty high order, but right now he felt the lack of siblings as Laura turned her wide, quiet gaze toward him.

They'd moved outside where a pair of shaky chairs huddled on a sad front porch. A bit dubiously, Laura tried out one. Archie tested the railing, then leaned against it, but standing over Laura didn't help that much. She had to be used to guys looming over her, he conceded. He leaned back to reduce the looming and waited.

And then waited some more.

Though there was silence between them, it was not quiet.

Voices on the street from the watchers. Voices from inside the house. Traffic noise. The occasional siren. And music. Almost all the time, he could hear music.

Even in January, the grass was green, less bright green, but still green. Some of the trees had leaves left. There were some less than pleasant smells wafting in from garbage cans waiting for pickup at the curbs. It was a Friday, so school-age kids had departed on a bus soon after they'd come outside. Funny that winter, even though it couldn't take over completely, still managed to spread a layer of bleak around. As the sun climbed, spreading its pale light over more of the street, the chill softened to damp cool.

A car backfire made him start. He pulled his attention back to the present to find Laura had stretched her feet out between the slats and closed her eyes, her head resting against the peeling back of the chair.

His gut clenched, and his fingers tried to curl into fists as longing hit him hard. What would it be like to wake to that face? To see the slow lift of lashes and the lips curving up—lips waiting to be kissed—

She sighed, and her eyes opened, not sultry, just sleepy and a bit grumpy. She rubbed her eyes, then her face, pulling her legs in. She stretched like a cat, and then her gaze caught his, and she froze.

Her expression didn't change, but her pupils dilated, and he saw her pulse ramp up. Had he thought it was cool? It wasn't. His mouth dried. A good thing because he wanted to say something he shouldn't. He should look away. He couldn't.

A car door slammed behind him, and she jumped, giving him her profile to study. Her lips trembled, but before either of them could speak, a voice called her.

"Laura."

The guy only said her name, but it drew Laura up from her chair and turned them both toward it.

"What's wrong?" Her voice was flat, her body braced for bad news.

"LaFon's been in an accident."

The guy didn't hesitate or pull his punches. Archie respected that, even though it made him want to punch something. The guy maybe.

"He's dead," Laura stated it, even as the color drained from her face. "What happened?"

"He was crossing a street." The guy came up the steps and took Laura's hands in his.

"Hit and run."

He nodded. "Witnesses said the car never braked."

She pulled her hands free and turned away from them both, her arms wrapped around her middle.

The desire to comfort her, to hold her shocked him.

"I can drive you home," the guy offered.

Archie didn't move a single cell, but the guy's gaze shifted toward him as if he sensed Archie had wanted some cells to move.

She turned around, her lips twisting. "Thanks, Frank." Her gaze shifted to Archie. "Archie can drive me home."

"Archie?" Frank's brows rose.

"This is my brother, Frank," she offered. "Archie is a friend of Becca's."

Frank nodded, but his gaze was still narrowed. Now that he knew, Archie realized he should have seen the resemblance to Zach, and to a lesser degree, Alex.

"No one was at the house," Frank said.

"Zach is inside with Alex." She half turned toward the street and stopped. "My car is in the alley."

Frank hesitated, his gaze moving between Laura and Archie, then he held out his keys. "We can trade back later."

Archie took the keys. Laura dug in a pocket and handed him hers. "Thanks."

As she moved to pass him, he gave her an awkward half hug. His gaze shifted to Archie. He looked like he wanted to ask or order. Gunn wasn't sure which.

"Thanks. I'll see you at the house, Laura."

It was very close to an order. Frank, Archie recalled, was FBI. Frank hesitated once more, then turned and entered the house. And he was alone with Laura. A still shocked, still reeling Laura, but there was something else.

Now her steady gaze was a steely, "We're gonna talk."

7

LAURA DIDN'T SPEAK as he held the door for her, stayed silent when he climbed in the driver's seat, and eased her brother's car through the cluster of emergency vehicles.

He didn't have words for how much he didn't want to leave without knowing what had happened to the necklace, but he was nothing if not pragmatic. If it had been found by Henri's attacker, it was already gone. If it hadn't been found, it wasn't going to be found until Henri told them where it was. His last sight, before he turned a corner and left Henri's street behind, was of a stretcher being loaded into the ambulance.

Looked like, for now, that Henri was alive. He opened his mouth to ask her to let someone know to post a guard—and closed it. Zach might not know Archie's story, but he'd been a cop and could add. As long as the cop wasn't dirty, Henri had a chance.

And so did he. If—

He glanced at the silent girl next to him.

Shock still kept the color from her face. Her lips were tightly compressed. Her hands clutching each other. After a small hesitation, he reached over and covered her clenched hands with one of his.

They were icy, clammy.

"I'm sorry," he said.

She licked her lips. "I am, too."

She glanced at him, and the grief in her eyes made him want to slam on the brakes and take her in his arms.

"He was a good man. A good partner. Good at saving lives."

Gunn wasn't sure what to ask or say, so he waited, his gaze moving from her to check behind them. They could have picked up a tail back there. What was one more car in that mess?

He made some random turns. Watching for trouble, waiting for Laura to ask.

"Is there a connection?"

She'd have had a lot of practice at channeling calm in a crisis, but Gunn was still impressed.

"It's possible," he admitted. "We were probably followed last night," he reminded her.

"My dad's house..."

He didn't speak, just waited.

"We should go to the morgue," she said, managing to surprise him.

She'd said that before, but...

"Okay."

She gave him the next few turns. Take a right. Take a left. Not that street. This one.

"Are we being followed right now?"

"I'm not sure," he admitted. If they were, they were hanging back. Not being obvious. Or they'd been waiting near the alley entrances. "We might have lost them by taking this car."

"Why kill him?" The words came out with suppressed passion. "He didn't have anything to do with this."

"He was there." Gunn hesitated. "You said that your hit and run said ogre, too. Did he say anything else?"

She bit her lip. And then she shifted to look at him. It was not a comfortable examination. He was, he knew, being assessed. Could she trust him? It wasn't easy to endure, because he wasn't sure she could trust him. There was more on the line, more than his past, or their lives. He didn't want to poke that bear or think about it. But he felt the risk of being this close to her. He had tried this before and failed. And in the end, she'd have decided for herself. Words from him or anyone else were useless right now.

Slowly, as if she had to tell it all, she began to speak. "He asked me if I was a real blonde and I asked him if he would believe me if I said I was. He had always liked blondes, he said. And then he moved." She drew in a breath. "Must have hurt like hell because he was busted from head to toe. But he sort of offered the beads. They were covered in, well, everything they could be covered in."

She looked away for a moment.

"Take them, he said. Pretty girl should have beads. They'll bring you luck, he said. Not lucky for him, but LaFon said it would make him feel better. So I took them. I mean my uniform was already covered in crap, too. So I did. I...promised I'd hang on to them. For luck."

Gunn bit back the impulse to ask more, drill for more. She needed to hold onto to the thread of it.

"Then he said ogre. *Hunt ogre.* At least that is what it sounded like."

"Hunt?" He allowed himself the small question.

"Yeah, it didn't make sense, but neither did ogre."

She was quiet for a whole block, and he had to fight with himself again to stay silent and wait for her.

"I told him we'd do what we could and then he said 'baby,' at least that is what it sounded like. I repeated it, and then he looked worried maybe or scared. He told me to be careful. And then..."

She stopped, and Gunn almost broke the steering wheel gripping it.

"Treasure. He said, 'treasure.' Very clearly, no question."

"Treasure," Gunn repeated the word, feeling it echo through his mind.

"He flatlined right after that. There was nothing we could do for him."

She sounded exhausted and sagged in the seat with her eyes closed.

"Did you tell anyone else?"

She opened her eyes, giving him a wary glance.

"Was anyone else at the scene close enough to hear?" he amended.

"We signaled to the on-scene cop. He was the one in the car last night. The one who stopped to see if we were okay outside the restaurant."

"I remember."

"He asked if he said anything about who hit him and LaFon —" her voice broke, and it took her a few seconds to go on— "told him it was an ogre. But that's all."

Except she ended up on the news wearing the beads. Who else had seen them? Had that single word ended up in a police report? And who had seen that?

"Ogre," he repeated. He couldn't fault her on her hearing, because Henri had said the same thing.

"Ogre," she agreed. "And now I've told you my story, it's your turn."

"Yes," he agreed heavily. He had to take his hand off hers to reach into his inside pocket. He extracted a partially folded letter-sized envelope and handed it to her.

With a wary glance at him, she opened it and took out a photograph. They paused at a light long enough for him to watch her expression as she took it in.

"But that's—" she stopped.

"Is it the same?"

"I can't be sure, but it looks like the same beads."

It was interesting that she saw them as Mardi Gras beads and not as an obviously expensive necklace.

She looked at him. "This is from a collection?" Her eyes widened. "Treasure? It's all...missing? Stolen?"

"Until I saw those around your neck the other night, I'd have sworn—and I'm not the only one who believed this—that this collection had been completely destroyed."

"Destroyed?"

"Seventeen years ago." He had to pause to steady his voice. Even now he could feel the shock of it vibrate through him. "September eleventh."

He heard her shocked inhale.

"The twin towers."

"The twin towers," he echoed.

"Who—" She stopped.

How, he wondered, had she known there'd been someone and not just the "treasure?"

"My brother." He said it flatly but heard the echoes of old pain flooded back in a tide.

The pause felt long, but this time it was her hand that covered his fist where it rested on his knee. Her hand felt cold but still managed to generate warmth as her new grief and his old grief forged something between them he couldn't think about right now.

"There," she said.

For a moment his brain fumbled, then he remembered. The morgue. Where—

"The one that looks like the front of a funeral home."

He looked at her, a brow arched, and she nodded.

"Yes, it was. We're supposed to be getting a nice, shiny new morgue but so far..." She shrugged. She reached for the door handle, but Gunn grabbed her arm.

"Wait," he said. He clambered out and studied the street behind and ahead of them, but his gut wasn't twitching—other than with fear for this woman and worry about her effect on him. Finally, he went to her side and opened the door, extending a hand for her.

"Let's go meet my sister," she said.

———

Archie studied Hannah for so long that Laura had to resist the urge to tell him Hannah was taken. She didn't know why he needed so much time. They were all pretty much alike.

"You're both very different, aren't you?" Archie finally said.

Hannah arched her brows and gave Laura a "we have to talk" look before leading them back to her "office." It was a desk in the corner of one of the examining rooms. There were stacks of file folders on her desk. She picked up the top one, and opened it, bit her lip, and looked up at them.

"I only had time for a quick look at your victim," she said, giving Laura a veiled look of annoyance this time. "He's not on the list for an autopsy."

Laura had a feeling she'd only agreed to meet them so she could get a look at Archie. Rumors would be swirling in the sibling network, but they'd all be wrong, she thought with a sigh.

"We're trying to find out more about him," Laura explained

when Archie didn't speak. So, no one had claimed his body. "Do we have a name?" LaFon was the one who had secured and bagged his personal items that night.

Hannah lifted a bag that was also lurking on her desk clutter. "I didn't log in his personal items." Her gaze ran down the list. "No wallet."

"That could have been stolen before we got there." Laura sighed. In that neighborhood that was more than likely. If he'd had a wallet. "So no ID?"

Hannah frowned at the list. "Says here the victim was Hebert LeBlanc. There was a social security card in one of his pocket's."

Laura's lips twisted. "Two of the most common names in Louisiana."

"Did you notice anything unusual, anything that would give a clue to where he'd been?" Archie finally spoke.

Hannah hesitated. "Well, obviously he had a lot of vehicular-related injuries."

"But," Laura prompted.

"He had a bite on his leg."

"A bite?" Archie's voice left the neutral zone.

"Without an expert, I can't say for sure..." Hannah hesitated again, then sighed. "It looked like it could be a gator bite."

———

Hannah "let" them see Hebert's body. He'd been cleaned up after he arrived at the morgue. He wasn't as old as Laura had thought. She had, she realized now, slotted him into the home-less, possibly alcoholic, category, but with the muck gone there were none of the usual signs of alcoholism. This did not bump him into a prosperous category. His nails hadn't had a manicure for a while—or ever—and his hair needed a better cut.

Laura looked away while Hannah zipped the bag down

and exposed the bite. That she did study. Not that it provided much insight. She'd seen a wide variety of injuries but had not yet encountered an alligator bite. Something to look forward to.

"According to the tech who processed the victim, the wound was wrapped in a tee shirt, and he cleaned off a lot of algae in and around the wound." Hannah flipped through the pages, then looked up. "That's all that seemed interesting."

"Algae?" Archie arched a brow.

"Like swamp algae?" Laura asked.

"Louisiana has algae in a lot of places," Hannah said dryly. "Looks like the tech saved some samples, but I can't send them out for testing without authorization." Something in Archie's face perhaps prompted her to add, "Our budget is pretty sad. Unlike TV shows, we don't get to go off testing things that look curious whenever we want."

"I understand," he said. "Is there any chance we could get one of the samples to test ourselves? I might know someone at UNO..."

Hannah hesitated, but it wasn't as if nothing ever walked out of here without permission. Only last spring a crazed killer had waltzed in, stolen evidence, and strolled out again. Hannah set both the file folder and the property list down on her desk and left. Laura looked away as Archie used his phone to snap photos of each page of the folder, and the cover letter for Hebert's personal belongings. His phone was put away and the file closed by the time Hannah came back. She set the samples down and turned to Laura, her back to Archie.

"It's a pity your victim didn't say anything before he died."

"But—" Laura hesitated, but she'd gone too far.

"There's nothing in the file," Hannah pointed out with a frown.

"Well, maybe no one wanted to write down ogre."

Archie had shifted so he was part of their little group again, and the samples were gone.

"Ogre?" Hannah frowned.

"That's what it sounded like to me and LaFon—" Her voice broke as she said his name. "He told the beat cop, but more as a joke." She took a shaky breath. There'd been more. Had LaFon told someone—the wrong someone—the rest of the conversation? He hadn't seemed to take it any more seriously than she had, but what if someone had asked him? Only the three of them knew Hebert had said anything that night. It was a sad, weird story with beads and an ogre. Another war story.

"Maybe the cop didn't write it down," she suggested. He was young, and all he'd been handed was ogre. Fast way to get teased if he had written it down. He'd been there last night but before they were followed...she was too tired to be paranoid and too tired to not be. Too tired and too...sad. LaFon. His hit and run might have nothing at all to do with the beads.

"I wonder..." Hannah's voice trailed off.

"What do you wonder?" Archie's voice was carefully bland as if the answer didn't matter at all.

"Well, maybe he was saying *Auger*." She spelled the word, then repeated it with a more French pronunciation.

Laura's eyes met Archie's. "Ogre. *Auger*."

"Does that name mean anything to you?" Archie asked, his brows drawn together.

Hannah half shrugged. "You should talk to Frank."

Frank. Laura rubbed the ache between her brows. The one thing they did not need was a link to organized crime. But—she thought the family knew all the Family names, thanks to Alex's wife, Nell.

"Not a local family," Laura protested, though half-heartedly. She was not an expert on crime in New Orleans or anywhere else. She was EMS, despite the high number of law enforcement professionals in her family. She had been called to crime scenes, of course, but only when the victims were still alive. The law enforcement part she avoided. It was probably Freudian or something.

Hannah hesitated, her gaze flickering to Archie, then repeated, "Ask Frank."

8

WAS LAURA IN DANGER? Archie considered the events of the last twenty-four hours, trying to figure out an answer to that question.

Two people connected to Hebert LeBlanc were now dead.

Someone had followed them last night. But with what intent?

Laura had been the one wearing the beads on TV, and he wouldn't have noticed them if the camera hadn't zoomed in close. He'd felt a chill at the shape of the Krewe badge, and the streetlight had caught the diamond, making a modest flash even with the dirt obscuring part of it. And he wouldn't have been here to see her or the necklace if not for the strange tip he'd received...

Was her partner dead because of what he'd heard Hebert say? If he was, then Laura was in danger.

Ogre. *Auger.*

Had someone acted to make sure the name stayed out of any official report? What about the beat cop, the only other person who'd heard ogre mentioned? Archie could make the case for the cop to be clean and too embarrassed to enter the word ogre into his report—or dirty for not entering it. No way to know without asking someone with access to the report.

Hannah Baker wanted them to talk to their brother Frank, but Archie wasn't sure he wanted more Bakers involved. In fact, he'd like to reduce the number of involved Bakers to zero. Archie glanced at Laura. How did he ease her out? Would she be wise enough to be careful? Not that being around him—if the beads were *the* beads—was any safer. But at least he knew there was danger and was watching out for it.

"I'm not super thrilled about calling Frank," Laura said, breaking into his thoughts.

"Oh?" He glanced at her, noting that she looked tired and that it did nothing to lessen her appeal. He'd been startled by how alike—but how different—the two sisters were. One he thought attractive, the other was more interesting for some reason he couldn't define, and he needed to get clear from her as quickly as he could because interesting was also distracting. He'd told her his part, but not all of the story, and if something happened to her—the jolt to his gut surprised him. The scent of her seemed to fill the car putting his desires at war with his need to find out the truth. Part of him wanted to get away, part of him wanted to—

"Why?" he asked.

"We won't get just Frank." Her profile was all clean, sultry lines with her lips compressed. She glanced at him. "I haven't... fully disclosed. They won't like that."

And they wouldn't like him. He nodded. He didn't do popularity contests, but it was a good thing he couldn't want more from Laura, so what her brothers thought of him couldn't matter either. They couldn't matter, he repeated to himself. Because...

If the beads were the real deal...

If the beads were not just the real deal, but the same deal...

If...

Then he was the last person Laura Baker should be around.

Because he was gonna kick up the anthill good and hard.

He was going to find out what really happened.

Or die trying.

And he was never going to get the girl.

———

Laura wasn't worried about Hannah or Ingrid spilling to the brothers. None of them did if they could help it. It was an unspoken pact stretching back to when they'd all lived together in the same house. Their pact didn't mean she wouldn't be grilled by the sisters when she was no longer with Archie.

Odd how that gave her a pang. Usually, she was better about keeping her distance so she wouldn't get pangs when a guy walked away. Or was run off by her brothers. She stole a glance at Archie. His hands gripped the steering wheel, his jawline was set in grim lines, and he stared straight ahead as if he could pull the answers he wanted out of the humid air.

They may have exchanged some glances at various times today, but she could feel him physically and emotionally withdrawing to some place inside. Or was it a time?

September 11, 2001.

They all lost their innocence that day, but the families that lost loved ones—that was an extra level of pain. She saw loss and grief every day in her work, but always from the outside. She'd been too young to remember her mom. LaFon was the closest death that had personally intruded into her adult world. They were friends, and she'd never been to his house. Never met his family, and he'd only met the Bakers they encountered at work. Their friendship had existed in a work bubble. It was shocking to realize it now. They'd worked so closely together in such extreme circumstances that their association felt intimate even though they'd never hugged or touched hands.

They clocked out and went away from each other until the next shift.

Oh, she knew things about him. Chat filled the spaces between calls.

He wasn't married either.

He loved his mom. His dad had died before he was born.

He was a Saints fan. Was conflicted about the Brass. It was a cold sport for a fan raised in the South.

He liked to read when they were at the station.

He liked his women tall and built.

He laughed when she called him sexist.

He liked to tease.

He used humor to deal with the trauma they faced every shift.

He'd met someone. He was sure this was the one.

She was the tenth? Eleventh one?

Laura had lost count.

Just like her, he'd wanted to find love, have a family, give his mom grandkids to play with.

Kids liked him.

Almost everyone liked him. He drew people to him.

He was steady and calm in a crisis. Not just good at what he did. He was great at it. Who might die because someone decided LaFon's life didn't matter?

She'd get a new partner and the gap his loss had left would close, though the scar of it would remain. But life did go on. There was no escape from that truth. Anger stirred inside her. Life could pause for a while, give you time to grieve and—well, it shouldn't just roll on, roll over the hole.

She released a silent, shuddering sigh. This wasn't the time for grief or for tears. If she cried—she slanted another look at

Archie. He'd drop her home as soon as he could. Did he hold the key to finding out how who killed LaFon? Oh, she knew LaFon wasn't his primary interest. How could he be? But if it was all connected?

She'd never had the urge to dive into the law enforcement side of the family business.

Until now.

The question now was, did she really want to? Or was it loss, grief, and guilt that fueled the longing? And if she did dive in, would she help or hinder? She did not want to get in the way of the justice Archie wanted to deal out. There was something tough and inevitable about him. The kind of good-guy ruthlessness she saw in her brothers and her dad.

She'd put her money on him getting to the bottom of the murk and delivering a good smackdown. It wouldn't bring LaFon back. Nothing would. She didn't know if justice would help ease the knot in her chest, but she wanted it. Oh yeah, she wanted it for him.

The car stopped, then Archie angled into street parking. She looked around, then at him, unable to hide her surprise.

"This is the closest I could get to the Bon Ton," he explained.

Bon Ton? Her brows shot up.

"I'm hungry. Thought you might be, too."

"Very." She felt guilty about that, but she was hungry enough to feel shaky as she waited while he opened her door for her. She'd never have tagged him for Bon Ton, but how would she know his type after one dinner and a crime scene? She looked at her watch. "Do you have a reservation?"

"My friend told me if you go late your chances are better."

So that's how he'd heard about it. Bon Ton was one of those places that didn't need to advertise. Their clientele was old and mostly local. She and LaFon—her thoughts stuttered for a moment—had responded to a heart attack there once. Mrs.

Pierce had given them both a bread pudding to go. Her mouth watered just thinking about it. Guilt stabbed again, but not eating wouldn't help LaFon.

Archie cupped her elbow, steering her toward the striped awning. Inside, she looked around curiously. She hadn't had time for gawking last time she was here. Crisp, white tablecloths, brick accents, and subdued lighting, oh, and the smell of great food. Yeah, she remembered that.

Not all the tables were full, so she had hope, but just as the hostess materialized in front of them, a voice reached out from a corner table.

"Archie? Archie Gunn?"

Laura looked toward the voice. The man rising to greet Archie was in his fifties, had once been in decent shape, but that shape had succumbed to food and booze. If he hadn't already had a heart attack, he was on his way to one.

His smile was hearty, but his gaze was wary and he'd lost color under his ruddy complexion.

"Auguste." Archie took the man's outstretched hand, but a whiff of cool wafted out with the single word.

"I haven't seen you since—" Auguste stopped, more white leaching the color from his cheeks.

"The funeral," Archie agreed. He glanced at Laura. "Laura, this is Bernard Auguste. This is Laura Baker."

Auguste nodded, his genial smile still loaded with lots of fake. His lashes flickered, and she wondered if he already knew her name—first or last.

Auguste hesitated, then changed the subject. "What brings you to New Orleans?"

He was local, Laura decided, his accent a little Cajun.

"A friend is getting married."

Auguste nodded, his smile turning fixed as his gaze strayed

toward Laura. If he recognized her from her brief appearance on the news...

"Your daddy Zach Baker?"

She nodded, letting her expression do the inquiring for her.

"Deposed him a couple of times. He was a good witness."

This did not sound like a compliment.

"Defense lawyers used to hate that about him," she said, bringing out her own fake smile.

Auguste's brows arched, and he gave a surprised chuckle. "You're your daddy's girl."

Again, she did not sense a compliment, though his gaze did an admiring, but slimy run down, then back up.

Jerk.

An uncomfortable pause was finally broken by Auguste.

"I'd invite you to join us, but we just finished," he said, gesturing at the table.

He wasn't alone, but the shadows hid whoever it was, so Laura couldn't tell if his companion was male or female. He lifted a hand, and the hostess hurried over.

"Find them a table, hon," he directed.

There was a bit of charm there, but it was of the sleazy variety.

"It was nice to see you again, Archie," Auguste said. "Tell your parents—"

His voice trailed off as if he realized he didn't know if they were still alive.

"I'll tell them you said hello," Archie said. He let the hostess carry them to the far side of the room.

Laura didn't look back. She had a feeling she didn't want to see who had lunched with Auguste. Only when she was seated, facing the room, with a menu as a shield did she look in that direction. A waiter was clearing the table.

She didn't remember Zach ever mentioning Bernard

Auguste, but then he wouldn't have to her. She turned her attention back to Archie. He held a menu, too, though his frowning gaze was on the abandoned table.

"You knew he'd be here," she said.

He tensed, then his head turned in her direction.

"I'm sorry about that."

"I will—" She stopped before "survive an introduction to a sleazy lawyer" passed her lips. It was not a good day to talk about surviving. Or not surviving. "It's all right. People around here don't really want to kick up the Baker anthill."

Her look felt wry. It must have looked it because Archie grinned, his face losing its grim severity. He sobered, hesitated, then sighed.

"He was the one who hired Rob to guard and transport the collection." He rubbed the bridge of his nose. "I told Rob not to get involved with that...but the money was good. Real good."

"I see." At least, she thought she did. "Do you think he... faked them before your brother picked them up?"

Archie shook his head with decision. "Rob wouldn't have fallen for that. And he had his own guy look over each piece before he left with them."

She considered this. People, even "own guys" could still be bought.

As if he read her thoughts, he shook his head. "Rob took extra care. He built the company. He was the company. He was... good at what he did."

And Archie had admired his big brother, looked up to him. Only now was she beginning to realize what a shock seeing the beads must have been to him. Seventeen years. Her sister-in-law Nell had told her that the tearing shock of loss eventually dulled to a throb that sometimes pulsed when memory jabbed the spot. Nell had learned to live with the double loss of her parents, but finding out their hidden history had definitely jabbed at her old pain.

And Zach, well, he was still dealing with his brother's unexpected return from the grave. He tried to hide it, but it was there in his expression at odd moments and sometimes when he looked at his brother, pleasure and pain wrestled in his eyes.

The shadow in Archie's eyes told her that his pain hadn't just been jabbed. It had been slammed into a brick wall.

Because she didn't know how to help Archie, she went for a distraction. "So when do you think they were switched?"

He hesitated. "Maybe they weren't switched. Maybe...Rob was dead before the tower fell."

The jolt of these words sat her back in her chair.

"Murdered?"

"It's the only thing that makes sense."

"A perfect murder," she murmured. "But..."

His lips twisted. "An unexpected bonus. I wonder what the scene would have looked like..." His voice trailed off, and his big shoulders rose and fell in a sigh. "With or without the towers falling, Auguste got his insurance payment. If that necklace hadn't turned up on your neck on the news, and if I hadn't happened to be watching..."

It would have remained the perfect murder.

She wanted to protest, but the last word Hebert had spoken kept the words back.

Treasure.

9

OTHER THAN ORDERING, Laura didn't say anything until she'd cleaned her plate and pushed it back. She caught Archie watching her and gave him a rueful, almost smile that caused an odd twinge around his heart. The feeling puzzled him. He'd been married twice, so nothing should be new, but this was.

"This is why people bring food," she said.

Archie arched his brows.

"After..." She trailed off and looked away. "Thank you. It was very good. I feel better." Her gaze returned to meet his. "And I feel guilty for feeling better."

Guilt was a strange beast. It struck without warning, stealing pleasure from simple moments. The better man had died. He knew that, accepted it. Rob had always been so large, so alive. It was a pity Hailey hadn't remarried, but Rob was hard for anyone to follow. Impossible, he acknowledged heavily. He did his best, but he felt how wrong it was as each anniversary, each life event that had passed for his brother's kids. He had known their father in a way his brother's kids never would. His mom's shadowed gaze haunted him as each anniversary approached, and he felt his dad's quiet pain as they carefully didn't talk about Rob.

Survivor guilt. He knew the term, had lived with it, around it, and in it for the last seventeen years. His second ex had told him she couldn't live with Archie's shadows anymore. Was this what she meant? He thought he was okay until this blew up in his face. The wound that time had quieted felt all raw and angry, throbbing in his chest again. He fought against rubbing the spot that throbbed and realized his hands were fisted. He forced his fingers straight, struggling to slow his breathing.

"Do you think—no." Laura shook her head. "Sorry, none of my business."

"What?" He was glad for the distraction.

"Would he have...survived..." She let the question trail off, giving him a chance to let it lie.

"He was in the second tower." He'd called Rob, but the call had rolled over to voicemail. Was he already dead? "We didn't know..."

"No, we didn't know," she agreed. She hesitated, then added, "I can close my eyes and still feel the shock of wondering what had happened. Wondering what was going on until..." She licked her lips, and it seemed to Archie that she made herself add, "Until the second tower was hit."

"We didn't know," he agreed. He'd told himself, his parents, Hailey, and the kids this. It didn't help because what he wanted was to rewind the clock and have it not happen. To go back and do something, anything differently so that Rob didn't die. But he had died. It happened, and nothing could change that. So he'd turned his mind to getting justice for Rob, for all those who had died. Had they got it? It didn't feel like it. Was this how all survivors felt? That it wasn't enough, that it would never be enough? He forced himself to look at the question. If he found out that the collection had survived, if he found out who had it, would that be enough? And what if he didn't get all the answers? What then? Could he live with not knowing? Could he live the rest of his life in his brother's larger-than-life shadow?

Unbidden, a memory came to him. He'd said something to Rob about justice, about why he wanted to be a cop. Rob's face had twisted into something not Rob-like.

"Only rich people get justice, little brother."

Perhaps something in Archie's face had registered because Rob had punched him lightly on the shoulder, the unsettling expression in his brother's eyes changing to wry. "You go for it, just...don't expect too much. People, well, justice isn't all black and white. People aren't either."

He'd looked like he wanted to say more, but instead had shaken his head and turned away.

Odd, he'd remember that now. Of course, he'd never seen Rob again and had other things to think about. For some reason the memory left him feeling unsettled and—

He heard a soft ping of a text arriving. Laura pulled out her phone.

"It's from Zach. He wants us to meet him at Henri's."

"Does he—" Archie halted the question. If her old man had said more, Laura would have told him.

"He doesn't like long texts," she explained.

The bill had been paid. There was nothing to stop their leaving, but Archie found it took an effort to rise and pull out Laura's chair. She was right. The food had helped. But so had this place. And the woman he'd shared it with.

———

It was quieter around Henri's house, though patrol cars lurked at the front, and back of, the house. Her gaze lingered thoughtfully on the CSU van. So Ingrid was still here. Alex's truck was gone. Zach was still alpha, it seemed.

Had someone found the beads? Had Henri regained consciousness enough to tell who had attacked him? Was this attack about the beads? Where they were?

She almost wished they were gone forever. But, she glanced at Archie as they went up the half-broken walk, never knowing wouldn't help, even if finding out might be worse. His brother was dead. How much would it change anything to know he'd been murdered? As he'd pointed out, the crime scene was gone. And learning the provenance of the beads? She couldn't see how that would help either. After seventeen years, they could have changed hands several times. Whoever had taken them—assuming these were the same beads—would have taken care to keep them hidden. That was the problem with stolen goods. One couldn't admit one had them or show them off. For some, possessing was, apparently, enough.

Which brought her around to wondering, what was the point of stealing them if the thief couldn't sell them or even show them to anyone? It would be tough to explain possessing something that was supposed to have been destroyed. But, if someone had murdered Archie's brother, they wouldn't have known what was going to happen. If those planes hadn't crashed into the twin towers, the collection would have been known to have been stolen, known to have blood on them. In the movies and on television, thieves had a buyer lined up before the theft or soon after. What if the thief and murderer had a plan, but it went sideways when the towers fell? Was honor among thieves enough when one side of the pact knew that the other side was a killer, too?

How would the so-called destruction of the collection have changed the dynamics of them as stolen goods? Had it cleaned up the trail for the thief? The collection would be gone. No one had been looking for any of it for seventeen years. Not only had it been the perfect murder, but the perfect crime.

Until the beads turned up on the news around her neck. Okay, so that was bad. It would be hard to explain how someone came by any of the items in the collection, but Hebert was dead. He couldn't tell anyone where he got the beads.

It was still possible the collection had been swapped before Rob left New Orleans. She could see why Archie wouldn't believe that, but she knew her city and had had a lot of experience with its seedy underside.

So, if the collection had been swapped out, then someone here did it. Had Rob been set up to be the fall guy for the theft? So both Auguste and Rob's expert would fall under suspicion. But how had Hebert got his paws on the beads? He couldn't have been telling her to go treasure hunting. He'd almost looked afraid there at the end. For some reason, this brought back to her mind the man she'd seen in the crowd.

"There was a man," she said, taking her thoughts into speech as they mounted the weather-beaten steps.

Archie stopped rather abruptly, his brow arching again. It must save him a lot of effort, that. Instead of having to think up questions, he just popped a brow up. She wished her brows didn't insist on working together. The single brow pop would have been nice to deploy against her brothers...

"What man?" Archie asked, probably because she hadn't answered.

Laura reined in her rabbit-hole dive of brows and brothers. "At the accident scene. He was sort of at the edge of the crowd." She shivered involuntarily. "A real creep."

That wasn't quite right, because he'd been dressed in a suit and all. "Not a nice man," she qualified. She'd gotten more experienced with criminal types at Alex's wedding. His wife was related to two local crime families. It had made the wedding tension different from the usual. "Someone who'd tried to paper over his bad, but his eyes gave him away. That's why I remember him," she added, with another shiver.

Archie frowned. "You haven't seen him since?"

"No, thank goodness. But I'd know him again." She said it with certainty while hoping she never had to find out if this were true. Memory, she knew, could alter without one even realizing it was happening.

Zach appeared in the frame of the screen door. His expression was a complex mix of cop and dad.

At this point she'd typically be shuffling her feet and hanging her head, but the day had started too early and contained too much drama for the hours that had passed. The good food had helped, but grief and worry and tired still jostled for primacy inside her head. All she wanted to know right now was if Zach had found the beads and were they *the* beads? She was too tired to figure out what happened next, but thankfully that was not her problem. This was Archie's circus, and once she'd done her part, she'd be happy to sink into the background. She slanted him a look and decided she might be a little sorry to see the last of him. And that was just because she was tired. Really tired. Because this guy was going to walk out of her life without a backward look.

Archie reached out to open the door for her and his gaze collided with hers. And just for a tiny moment, she saw heat flare in the depths and knew—or thought she knew—he might look back.

But he'd still walk away.

When she wasn't so tired, she'd be glad. The third time might be the charm for some couples, but Archie? He looked like a guy who thought he'd learned not to make some mistakes again.

Zach pushed from the inside, so the door came to meet Archie. He pulled it wide and waited for Laura to step inside before he followed her. Somehow this resulted in the brief brushing of his arm against hers, and she felt a sudden, urgent need for Archie to get on with the leaving.

"Did you find it?" she asked.

Her dad's brows arched at her tone, but he held up an evidence bag with the beads inside it. Archie was the one who took it, fingering the beads through the plastic.

"How?" Laura asked.

"Henri managed to tell me before they took him to the hospital. Was still the devil to find," he growled.

"Thanks," she said, resisting the urge to point out they wouldn't have had any of this if he hadn't handed it over to Henri in the first place. But...she'd had an amazing lunch. Zach had probably had a hot dog. She turned back to Archie. "Is it..."

His gaze lifted from the beads to meet hers. He sighed. "I'm not sure." His attention shifted to Zach. "Did Henri offer an opinion?"

Zach shook his head. "He was very interested, though. Said he needed to show them to someone."

"Someone?" Laura asked the question since she wasn't sure Archie's raised brow would work on her dad.

"He wouldn't tell me. Trade secret." Zach rubbed his tired face.

"I should run you home." The guilt was piling up. Had these beads been a factor in LaFon's death? It could have been a coincidence. Not every hit and run was a deliberate act. Sometimes people were just stupid, driving distracted, and then they panicked.

"I'll run him home," Alex's voice broke in from the doorway to the rear of the house. He must have pulled his truck around to the back alley.

Laura sighed. She took the evidence bag from Archie and

held it up. "Is this really necessary? Technically, these belong to me, and they weren't dropped here. They were hidden."

Alex hesitated. It was hard for him to make the case they'd be safer in the evidence lockup. She could see the struggle in his eyes. He didn't think they were necessary, but he didn't want her walking around with them until he knew more.

"Can I at least take them out?" Archie asked, breaking up the gaze stalemate. Alex hesitated again, then gave a sharp nod.

Archie broke the seal and dumped the beads out in his hand. He rubbed the "pearls" between his fingers, then lifted it so that the wooden Krewe badge and the stone were eye level. "Did Henri use a loupe on this?"

Now it was Zach's turn to hesitate. "He says he hadn't yet. Said even if that wasn't a gemstone, the age of the beads made the glass valuable."

"Did you believe him?"

Laura half frowned. Could what she thought was glass be a gemstone? Was the value in the age, in its composition, or the fact that it had resurfaced? Some or all of the above?

"Are they the same as the ones that went missing?" Zach was nothing if not persistent.

Archie's rueful gaze met hers. "I'm not sure. They look the same but..."

"They could be a copy?" Laura offered this, with a sideways glance at her dad.

He nodded. He reached into his jacket pocket and extracted the small booklet he'd shown to her. He flipped through the pages, stopped and held it up so they could all see it, holding the beads up at the same time.

"Rob showed me all the pieces in the collection, but it's been seventeen years." Frustration shone out of Archie's eyes.

"Seventeen years?" It was Alex who asked the question.

Laura glanced at Archie, got a small nod before she responded. "His brother Rob was killed on nine eleven."

Both Alex and Zach's eyes widened, then slid away. How had both of them managed to marry when they dealt with emotion so wonderfully well? She took the booklet from Archie and read the description under the beads. *Beads.* How about pearls, a giant blue diamond, and rare carved wood used for the Krewe badge. Holy crap. Had Henri been unsure about the beads' authenticity or been trying to figure out how to profit from the situation? She sighed. Would she ever know? Probably not because it was not her business. She'd sent her two questions out into the universe and got a yes, and a maybe. This story would go on without her.

"So who does own the beads?" she asked. If they were or weren't authentic, they did not belong to her. This was not a gift that Hebert had been qualified to bequeath.

"The insurance company," Alex said grimly. When he got a couple of looks, he added, "There would have been a claim and a payout."

Laura flipped through the pages until she found the introduction.

The collection is on loan from Cyria Auger Christophe of Vermillion Parish. *Auger. Ogre.* Had Hebert been trying to tell her who the beads belonged to or warning her about who had run him down?

She felt her dad's gaze homing in on her and looked up, aware she wanted to go into surly wary mode. Seriously, when was she going to quit letting Zach reduce her to thirteen with a look?

Alex held out his hand for the beads. Archie didn't hesitate to hand them over. That felt significant, though why eluded her. Alex frowned down at them for what felt like a long time. His moody gaze lifted.

"Well, Zach's already had one attempted burglary." He stopped, his frown deepening.

"Maybe that means he could stow them in the gun safe," Laura suggested. Alex's brows snapped together. "Do you want to take them home to Nell? Trust them to the evidence locker?"

"I should take them," Zach said firmly.

"I agree," Archie said unexpectedly. He glanced around. "If the necklace was the target, as soon as your people leave, someone will come and level this house looking for it."

"If it's the real deal," Alex pointed out.

"If they believe it is the real deal," Archie countered. "If it is a copy—"

"Who could tell us?" Zach asked.

Apparently, he didn't have a real expert on his contact list.

After a pause, Archie said, "I'll see if I can track down the insurance company adjuster who authenticated the collection the first time."

Laura almost asked how, but then she remembered she wasn't a cop. And was Archie? He was something, she conceded with a silent sigh. He was definitely something.

———

Laura was quiet as she drove away from Henri's house. Archie was surprised her old man was letting her drive him back to his hotel. If Zach Baker had had his own car, or if his son weren't on duty? Yeah, Laura would already be headed back to her dad's house.

Would she be safe there? That was the question that plagued him. Did the players—if there were players—have him in their sights? It was Laura who had worn the necklace on the news. He'd been with her, been seen with her, but was that enough to take the spotlight off her and put it on him?

He'd have warned her old man and her big brother, but as far as he could tell, they'd already figured it out—based on their level of deep unhappiness with him. He was sure Alex had opened his mouth to suggest calling a cab, but Laura beat him to the punch by offering to drive him. If her offer hadn't been back to the hotel, there would have been an intervention. Both had looked relieved at her removing herself from the risk zone.

He was relieved, too. It was better this way. If he were still alive in a couple of days, maybe he'd see if she'd be his plus one at the wedding. If this was over by then, he amended. It had been seventeen years in the making. Did he really think it could be resolved in a couple of days?

He glanced at Laura.

He could hope, couldn't he?

He made himself look away. Even if he'd cleared his wake of danger, that didn't mean he was any good for Laura. If he'd learned nothing else from his two failed attempts at marriage, it was how to walk away. Now would not be a good time to forget that hard-earned lesson. So can the hope, walk away without looking back. Trust in her many brothers and her dad to keep her safe.

"Could we drop off the samples with my friend before we head to my hotel?" he remembered to ask.

"Of course."

It was a small detour, and Archie made sure Laura was not in sight when he handed them off to his friend. And not just because this friend was female and didn't care about either of his divorces.

He returned to the car and thought Laura was asleep, but her eyes opened as soon as he tried the handle. She unlocked it, waited until he was inside and then turned them directly toward his hotel.

She signaled the turn, then pulled into the roundabout

in front. His hand curled around the handle as he arranged his expression to bland. There'd been that revealing moment outside Henri's house. He couldn't afford to do that again.

His mouth curved in a smile that was as bland as his gaze, and he shifted so he could see her.

"I don't know how to thank you," he said. She'd been more than kind, more than he deserved.

"I won't tell Becca, but Zach might," she said.

He almost flinched from the deliberate blandness of *her* face. Was he such a jerk that he wanted to see the regret he wouldn't let her see? He might be impressed that she was as good at hiding her feelings as he was. She couldn't hide the sweet curve of her mouth that had a hint of wistfulness around the edges though.

As if she sensed more from him, she added, "I'll be fine." Now her smile turned wry. "So overwhelmingly fine."

He had to laugh at this, the tension breaking as they both relaxed into humor. Before it could reform, he pulled the handle.

"Sorry," she said, hitting the unlock switch.

He started to push the door open. He should have been watching his surroundings instead of looking at Laura. Both rear doors opened, and two men were inside before either of them could react.

"Please close the door, sir. Miss Baker, take a right back onto the street."

If they sensed hesitation from either of them, they added to quell it, "Ms. Cyria wishes to speak with you, Miss Baker."

Archie stiffened, but hesitated, glancing at Laura. She was wide-eyed but calm. She shrugged.

"She could have phoned," Laura pointed out as she put the car back in gear.

Laura was right about that. If she'd called, he'd have gone. He wanted to talk to Ms. Christophe, too.

––––––––

It was not a good day to get hijacked. Laura looked at her watch, but the time didn't register. How much longer until her dad got an APB out on her car? She was to-the-bone tired. The kind of tired that made her want to sit down and wail like a little kid. It didn't matter that she was already sitting down because she had to drive, and she was too tired to cry anyway. Laura didn't even have a good whimper in her, so she followed the directions like a zombie on autopilot. A couple of her driving choices elicited some whimpers from her passengers, but her EMS shifts spent driving tired and fast helped her pull out the saves. Based on the half-hearted honking, road rage wasn't going to save them.

There were multiple sighs of relief when she turned into the curved drive of a lovely Garden District mansion. She studied the impressive facade and manicured surroundings through her haze of weariness.

It appeared, she decided, that she'd been kidnapped by someone with enough money to afford legal fees. She wasn't sure what that meant for her and Archie's continued survival. She exhausted enough to almost not care.

She got a second—or fifth—wind, okay, she'd lost track—as they mounted the shallow steps to double doors with elaborate paned insets. The pineapples might be an ironic choice since they were the symbol of hospitality.

Inside it was cool and dim, but not so dim she missed seeing the long stretch of polished wood floors and the march of antiques down each side.

No one spoke when their escorts stopped in front of tall doors that the two men moved to open. Laura half expected to get announced, but they ushered them in with gestures that were slight but somehow also managed to be threatening.

It was brighter in a room she took to be a sort of sitting room, based on the number of chairs and such scattered around. The space was littered with antiques that had to be navigated to get closer to their hostess who was vamp-posed in front of a fireplace that would have been cool to study in other circumstances. Off to one side, she could see what might be an atrium, based on the light level and enough palm fronds to make it into a small swamp. The air in the room trended toward swamp, too.

A blonde Morticia Addams posed in front of an elegant fireplace, her model long legs encased in tight, black leggings. Her white, possibly silk top, draped her body and arms as if it had been arranged to be dramatic. In profile, her nose was almost a pointed triangle, and the line of her hair was razor sharp. Red lips closed around a cigarette holder held in long fingers tipped with red. She eased the holder far enough out so she could send a stream of smoke into the air.

Her feet were long and white, the toes matched her fingers and lips, and her impossibly high-heeled sandals were so scanty as to be almost invisible, held in place with micro-thin straps of gold. At her feet were a couple of stuffed alligators. An interesting choice for such a mostly traditional room—one of the gator's tails flicked sideways, and Laura twitched against the longing to jump up on the couch. Not that it looked like it would last long if she made the leap. She wasn't sure it would survive her sitting on it—if asked.

The question of whether their hostess could walk in her ridiculous shoes was answered when she lowered the cigarette holder to an ashtray on the mantle, and then took three fairly stable steps in their direction. The two gators followed, one or both emitting their distinctive and unsettling rumbles.

Laura might have twitched again. This time their hostess's

pale blue eyes—which had been focused on Archie pretty much since they entered—turned in Laura's direction.

"Rudolf and Rachelle are perfectly harmless." She stooped, sweeping a hand along the first one, then the other gator's back. One or both of them rumbled again. She grabbed something from a tray and dropped it in each gaping mouth.

"Stay there," she murmured, whether that was meant for Rudolf or them was not clear. She gave each gator a final pat, then rose effortlessly. Considering the height of her heels, Laura was impressed at this win against gravity.

Of course, there wasn't a lot of body mass to lift. It was so fun to walk into a room and feel like a short troll. Not a single part of her generously shaped body missed out on the weight-shaming moment. It almost made her forget the gators. Though the memory of Hebert's bite chose to make a return, not helped when she looked down and saw Rudolf, or perhaps it was Rachelle's snoot almost touching her ankle.

"I'm Cyria Auger Christophe." There was an "of course, you know this already" tone to her languid voice. Cyria might have paused to catch her breath. Or she liked dramatic pauses.

Laura figured it was to catch her breath. The lungs in that narrow chest were probably the size of a kitten. Just then she shifted her pose, so the pause could be about what pose to do next. It looked like she chose forties bombshell, but what did Laura know?

"Please, sit down." Her hand swept out gracefully and then was drawn back to her side where it curved in an imitation of natural.

Archie may have hesitated before side-stepping and then cautiously lowering himself onto the dainty couch. It creaked but held, and he couldn't hide his relief. One of the gators rumbled and Cyria gave a tinkling laugh.

"Rachelle always has a weak spot for men."

The way Cyria's eyes were eating him up, Rachelle wasn't the only one. Laura had a feeling that Cyria could bite, too. But at least the lack of attention gave her time to sit down. The couch creaked again, a bit louder this time. Cyria's gaze drifted in her direction again and the thin, red lips curved up a tiny bit. Laura didn't know if it was too much effort or too much botox.

"How kind of you to visit me," she murmured, her voice managing to be both throaty and breathy with a swirl of a little girl. She sank into a wing-backed chair with sinister grace, all of her clothes and appendages seemingly arranging themselves in perfect lines by magical forces. Between them was a charming coffee table with an enormous silver teapot on an equally enormous silver tray. Exquisitely fragile-looking teacups huddled next to the usual sugar, milk, and lemon servers.

All of it, and their hostess looked like something from a movie. Laura studied Cyria and decided she could have stepped out of a cartoon. On that nasty thought, she felt slightly better.

Cyria leaned forward, and lifted the massive pot—Laura held her breath, but nothing dropped or broke—holding it over a cup.

"Tea?"

Laura didn't want tea, did not want to sip with the enemy but found herself nodding and murmuring, "Thank you."

Thank you. She'd just thanked her kidnapper. Either she was too tired to have good judgment, or the woman was an actual witch who had cast a spell over her.

It was a relief to hear Archie's decisive no. He didn't retract, even at her look of mournful disappointment.

"Can I get you something else?"

"No, thank you." Again Archie's voice was firm.

At least he'd thanked her, too. Laura felt somewhat better, even though she ended up taking the cup from the narrow hands that had rings on three of the five even narrower fingers.

Laura didn't even like tea.

At this angle, Laura got a closeup of the blingy necklace encircling a neck that was as long and white as the rest of her—and gave away her age. The neck was the mean girl of the body.

Laura, who had to guess ages a lot in her job, put her well into her fifties. She might be a bit mean with that estimate, but she couldn't help it. No one liked feeling like a short troll.

Cyria prepared a cup for herself, then leaned back and took what looked like a sip. Her lips briefly touched the edge of the cup but did not leave a smear of red when she moved it away. She briefly disturbed her perfect pose to set her cup and saucer on a tiny table next to her chair.

Not even a clink of china broke the silence. It was not a comfortable silence because of the kidnapping and the gators. Their hostess didn't help, though Laura thought she could take her. Of course, Cyria had people to do the taking for her. The question Laura had was what did Cyria want? Information or the beads? Both?

She rested her elbows on the arms of her chair and steepled her fingers, her clothing once more falling in line.

A person could go to church under that steeple, Laura thought, maybe a bit sourly. She fake sipped her tea, then set it down on the tiny table at her elbow, proud it didn't clink. She folded her hands together in her lap, fighting a wave of hot and sleepy, not to mention the picture of what she must look like in jeans and wrinkled tee, both scrambled into hastily this morning for the trip to Henri's house.

If Cyria's intention was to intimidate, she might have succeeded with another man. Laura stole a peek at Archie through her scraggly hair screen. His face was a blanker canvas than it had been facing down Zach the last couple of days. Had it been days? Or a day? Time was beginning to blur around the edges. She glanced at the cup and decided she needed the caffeine hit. She took more than a sip, so she wouldn't have to do it twice, then returned the cup to the table.

Cyria gave a tiny sigh as her gaze shifted in Laura's direction. "Miss Baker, Laura—may I call you Laura?" She didn't actually wait for permission, just went on, "I'm so grateful you agreed to visit me."

Laura was aware this put both of Archie's brows up. Her brows were too tired, but they rose in spirit.

Cyria gave a smile another try. It failed for lack of fine lines. Her pale gaze was turned toward Archie once more.

"Have we met before..."

"Archie Gunn."

"Gunn." Her eyes might have widened some. She repeated with shock in her tone. "Gunn..."

"I'm Rob's younger brother."

"Well," Her shoulders moved in surprise since it was a bit beyond the ability of her face. "How...interesting."

Had she really not known who Archie was? Laura couldn't decide. If she'd paled, there was no way to tell. Her blood all seemed to flow well out of sight.

Cyria's gaze met Archie's without flinching, but that might have been the botox.

How surface polite they all were. No one was asking, so no one was answering. Laura wanted to point out she hadn't agreed to visit, but if she ripped off the civil bandage, halted the pretense, then what? She might have joked about getting "mercy killed" after a long shift with LaFon—

Grief stabbed through the haze of tired, and she had to look down. Her hands trembled, and she clasped them together to hide it.

She didn't want to die. And no one had threatened to kill them, she admitted. There was nothing legal to get hold of, despite the nature of the "invitation" that had brought there them here. But the lady needed to quit the dancing around and get to the point.

What was the point?

It felt to Laura as if she'd lost the plot somewhere.

Cyria shifted ever so slightly in her chair, while somehow managing to stay dead center so that the chair's wings framed her perfectly.

"Your brother's loss...it was most...tragic."

It was possible she meant to sound sad.

Behind them, a door opened, and the wood creaked from a step. Cyria's gaze sharpened.

"Not now." Her tone was sharp, her expression complicated as it focused on someone out of their sight.

Laura half looked back, but the hall's shadows hid the figure, leaving the impression of a burly male frame before he stepped back and the door closed.

"He's too anxious to clear the tray," Cyria said with a weary sigh. "It's so hard to get help that knows what they are doing."

Help? Her impression of the figure was not that of a butler, though she couldn't have said why.

"I'm sure." Archie's tone was polite, but there was a faint crease between his brows.

For the first time, it seemed that Cyria rushed into speech. "You have to know I'm curious about the necklace." She gave a titter that was borderline nervous. "Of course it has to be a copy. But I was...wondering how you came by it?"

Her attention shifted back to Laura so suddenly, she half flinched back. One of Cyria's thin hands stroked the necklace around her neck.

Laura didn't rush into speech. For one thing, she didn't want to tell this woman anything, and for another, she wasn't sure she should. Or could, now that she thought about it.

"You saw the news?" Laura asked, mostly to stall.

"I didn't, but...a friend did and called me. The collection belonged to my late husband. It was a source of considerable..." her gaze flicked towards Archie, and it was possible she changed her words because of him, "consternation...when it was destroyed. But, of course, there were larger events playing out."

"And they were insured," Archie pointed out almost gently.

"Yes, they were insured, though really they were irreplaceable." She failed to hold Archie's gaze and turned to her teacup again. It almost seemed as if she steeled herself. "I quite liked your brother. He was...we were so sorry for your loss."

"As you said at the time." Archie's voice was blank as glass.

"It was my late husband's idea...well, that is old news, isn't it?" Her titter grated across Laura's nerves. "But...I would like, if there is a copy, I would be interested in purchasing it. It won't replace the collection, of course, but it was my favorite piece— and Raoul's. His favorite piece, I mean. Too."

Her carefully plucked brows rose in gentle inquiry over an attempt by her eyes to look soulful, as if this papered over her very thin explanation for her curiosity. Not to mention their hijacking.

Laura knew she sucked at lying but the truth...

"The police allowed me to study the necklace," Archie said. "I'm not sure it is the same."

It was the truth or at least a thin slice of it.

Cyria jerked slightly. "The police?"

"It was found at the scene of a murder."

Her brows did their best to shoot up. "A murder?" Her gaze moved between Laura and Archie.

This had, Laura feared, only postponed things. She sensed that what Cyria really wanted was the name of the man who'd given it to her. Why did that worry her? He was dead. Unless there was a trail to follow to the...treasure? Cyria might have a head start over Archie if she got the name. She didn't dare look at him or give Cyria any hint she knew anything. Not that Laura thought that she did know that much. To her, it seemed that the lady was more interested in Archie. Which was understandable and a little creepy.

As Laura watched their gazes politely clash, a tiny trickle of cold snaked down her back, pulling back the haze a bit. Everyone talked about seeing her on TV, but what would they have seen? Now she wished she'd watched the bit because— how believable was it that they'd all seen the necklace in the murky nighttime with only vehicle lights and the streetlights? Could they have recognized beads as *the* necklace? Had her screen time been long enough for that? It made sense her friends and family had recognized her, but could the beads really have been that distinctive? She'd have had to use resources to find out Laura's name. Resources that had followed them to the hotel? Was that even possible? Unless this was all a screen to get at Archie who had been staying at the hotel?

She felt unease spike, but what did it mean? If they hadn't recognized the beads from the TV bit then...

The memory of the creepy guy came back, further shredding her semi-comfortable haze. None of this made any sense unless someone had been following Hebert. Which actually made sense, she realized. Because someone had run him down. *Someone. Had run him down.* Why hadn't that someone secured the beads before she and LaFon—catch of pain there—arrived on the scene?

That question was more about an "if only" they had, she wouldn't be sitting here—

And maybe she wouldn't have met Archie.

She felt a third jolt hit her haze, one that almost brought her to full alert status.

Archie had seen the TV bit. Or claimed he had.

But what if he'd been in that crowd, too?

What if—

As if he sensed her looking, his gaze shifted toward her. The chill in them might have been a little terrifying. Laura picked up her teacup and lifted it to her lips, taking another, more cautious sip, then she grimaced. She was not a fan of teas, and this one was particularly bitter. She was rather proud—and surprised—by how steady her hand was as she set the cup back down and leaned back. Particularly, when the room seemed to soften around the edges. She tried to move a hand, tried to speak, but neither worked. Her lids started to lower of their own accord. As if from the moon, she heard Cyria say, "The poor girl is really quite tired, isn't she?"

Laura felt herself slip sideways as the lights went out...

———

Archie didn't understand what Cyria meant until Laura slumped against him. Tired or—

His chest tightened. Casually, his gaze never leaving Cyria's avid gaze, he groped for and found Laura's hand. She still had a pulse. He didn't let relief show on his face. If they sensed she was a weak point for him—

Though he didn't think they'd be walking out of this house. Funny how he still felt hope, felt the urge to fight for her life, for his—at least he had to get her out somehow.

He'd been in tight spots before. It always surprised him the mental clarity that followed that first frozen moment. He heard a rumble near his feet and glanced down. One of those damn alligators had its nose to his calf. No surprise now about how Hebert got that bite.

He tried to remember what he knew about alligators. It didn't take long because he didn't know much. Why should he? He lived in Colorado.

He considered several questions, but couldn't think of one that wouldn't up the risk. They were all pretending to get along. If he ripped the mask off...

"You're an unexpected bonus, Archie," Cyria said.

Had she really not known he was around? Hadn't Auguste called her after he left Bon Ton? Or had they had a falling out? Or was the bonus him being in the car with Laura? His head might have throbbed. Too many questions, too few answers.

Her gaze considered him with a mixture of cold assessment and a hint of lust. His stomach gave a lurch. Didn't want to be left out, he supposed.

"I really was so...fond of Robert."

Robert. The way she didn't use Rob made him wonder. Had she looked at his brother like this? Seventeen years ago, she'd have looked less like an aging bombshell and more—Hailey had still been trying to shed her latest baby fat. And so tired because Rob was working overtime on this deal—

His headache ramped up, and he flinched from the thought. Not Rob. He hadn't died with this, with this travesty of a woman on his conscience. Not Rob, he repeated to himself. But that memory cracked open a little more, as if he coated it and covered it with a mixture of grief and hero worship. Was it his first or second wife that called him a 'damn oyster.' Only, she'd pointed out, when he opened a little, there wasn't a pearl inside. Just more oyster.

He would have given a rueful grin at the thought. Pearls. Missing pearls. What did you call a pearl that was ugly?

He saw a hint of pleasure flicker in her eyes and knew he'd let pain leak out. She'd like it. She liked pain. She wanted to damage his memories of Rob, the brother who couldn't defend himself.

As if she sensed his retreat, her attention shifted to Laura. "She looks so uncomfortable. I can get someone to carry—"

It took almost more self-control than he had not to flinch, not to snap. His hand might have tightened around hers because she gave a small murmur, and shifted so that she rested against him more fully.

He waited until Cyria's gaze met his again. Let all the coldness in his soul chill his gaze. And all his indifference.

He gave her credit for not flinching or looking away.

"A pity," she said, her expression very similar to her two alligators.

10

"Laura?"

The voice was familiar. It was even a voice she sort of thought she liked, but she wished it would go away. She was so tired...

"Come on, Laura, open your eyes, sweetheart."

Sweetheart? That couldn't be anyone she knew.

"Don't..." The mumble startled her into lifting heavy lids. Had that been her voice? Her mumble? After a few moments, the blur cleared enough for her to recognize Archie. "Archie? What..."

She stopped because with returning consciousness came the awareness she was lying down. In a bed. Had she—had Archie—the heat of embarrassment helped push back the lethargy that had invaded her nethermost parts. She tried to sit up but needed Archie's help to manage it.

Another mumble turned into a groan.

She pushed her hair off her face and tried to swallow the dust filling her mouth. As if he knew, Archie held a cup to her lips. Her own hands clutched at it, and she gulped down at least half of the water it contained before lowering it a few inches.

This time she looked around with eyes that could see for the most part. The room they were in was fancy, the furniture all antiques. Heavy curtains framed long windows and wood gleamed softly in the low light. How had they—memories trailed sheepishly back, casting her apologetic glances before settling back into consciousness.

"I fell asleep?" Not just in the presence of a possible enemy but two gators? That was worse than thinking she and Archie had gotten horizontal and she forgot it. She considered this. Might be a tie between those two.

"I think you—" Archie said, with a hint of grim in his voice. "You were pretty tired."

"We're still—" It took too much effort to finish the sentence.

"Guests of Cyria? Yes."

Guests? She glanced around. Did he think someone was listening in? A more terrifying thought cleared a lot of the mist from her mind. "Zach—"

"I was..." He hesitated, then said, "I called him."

His gaze seemed to be trying to tell her something, so she nodded, even though she wasn't sure she understood. She looked at her watch, but the time meant nothing.

"How long have I...been sleeping?"

"Just a few hours."

Hours? It was incredibly creepy to realize how deeply asleep she'd been in what she considered enemy territory. That wasn't like her—at all. She recalled the bitter tea. Yeah, not like her. That's what Archie was trying to stop her from saying out loud.

"Why..." She stopped because the question she asked couldn't be asked if someone was listening. Why had they drugged her if they wanted answers? What were they waiting for? For Zach to deploy all the forces of the law to look for them? Because he would, with or without Archie's call.

Hours. She'd been asleep for hours, which meant...yup. She needed to go. Color crept up her face.

"Is there a bathroom?" She shouldn't be embarrassed. She had seven brothers who loved bathroom jokes. But this was... oddly intimate. They were close enough she could smell his aftershave, and she had her head turned to the side because she feared he could smell her post-nap breath. More color flooded her face.

"It's over there."

He helped her stand up. It took her a few steps to get her land legs back, but she made it. It was a very guest friendly ensuite—not to mention unusual for a house of this vintage. There was even a toothbrush in the wrapper. She used it without compunction. They owed her a toothbrush. With her face washed, her teeth brushed and her bladder happy, Laura felt better when she rejoined Archie. She was also more alert. She avoided the bed, however, making for two chairs flanking a small table near one of the long windows.

She sat with her back erect and asked, "So what happens now?"

Archie sank down in the other chair, but was back on his feet again when someone fumbled with the door handle. Or unlocked the door? Archie shot her a look, then moved, so he stood between her and whoever had pushed open the bedroom door.

With a quick, inner pep talk, Laura rose and peered around Archie. For a moment, the shadowed hallway hid the figure in the doorway, but then he stepped forward, and she felt an arctic waterfall cascade through her body.

It was the man she'd seen at the accident.

The man she'd hoped to never see again. And he had a gator on each side of him. That they were leashed was no comfort at all.

"Name's Bordelon," the man in the doorway said. "So, you're Zach's little girl."

His tone was civil, polite even, if Archie didn't look into his dead snake eyes or notice the ice dripping from the words. At his side, but out of sight of Bordelon, Laura's fingers curled around his, almost tight enough to hurt. He wasn't sure if she knew she'd grabbed his hand. Not that he blamed her. The guy was a creep with two alligators. And he'd told them his name. That didn't bode well for their survival.

"His favorite," Laura said, her tone hitting a place nicely between polite steel and humor.

Bordelon's thin lips twisted slightly. "Then I'm sure he'll be... glad when you are home again."

He stepped back and gestured for them to leave the room. Was he telling them they could go? Archie eased Laura forward, but kept himself between her and Bordelon. He didn't blame Laura for edging around the alligators. The two reptiles still grumbled when they drew even with them. Laura's hand jerked a little in his, but she didn't show any other sign of unease. Archie waited until they were clear of gators and this guy to meet his snake-eyed gaze.

Bordelon didn't flinch. He was probably armed with more than the gators. The edge of his mouth twitched into what might've en a sneer or a lame version of a smile.

"You look better than you did the other night." Bordelon's insolent gaze traveled down, then back up to meet Laura's gaze.

She met it with a coolly amused one. "That's not a high bar to get over." She took a half step forward.

"Does your old man have the necklace?"

She halted again. She regarded the lowlife in a way Archie hoped never got directed at him. It was hard to pinpoint why.

"The last time I saw the necklace was at Henri's house."

Truth rang in her voice because it was the truth.

It was Bordelon who caved first, if a flicker of the lashes was a cave. If he was what Archie thought he was, it was almost an admission of guilt. This time he let Archie and Laura get all the way into the hall before he spoke.

"Doesn't belong to you."

Laura stopped and glanced back at almost the same time as Archie. Funny that the blanker Bordelon's face got, the more threatening he seemed to be.

"No, it doesn't." She hesitated, then added gently, "I believe the insurance company owns it now."

The pale brows rose in genuine surprise. "You didn't—"

"Why yes, I did."

It was possible that Bordelon muttered, "Women" as they walked carefully down the stairs. It was long and slow, knowing those snake eyes were targeted at the center of his back the whole time. In the hall, the two goons who had hijacked them were standing on either side of the front door. There was a long pause, then one of them opened the door, revealing Laura's—no, Frank's—car where they'd left it a few hours before. They'd traded cars at the crime scene, he reminded himself, which now felt like it had been days, not hours, ago.

The other held out her handbag and his cell phone. Warily, Archie accepted both. Were they really going to let them leave?

"Ms. Christophe asked me to tell you she's sorry she's not able to see you off. She had business to attend to."

With the crawly feeling in the middle of his back growing, and some menacing growls from the gators just out of sight, Archie ushered Laura out the opening and into the passenger side.

He went around to the driver side, seeing without directly looking, at both men who now stood in the opening watching them. The keys still hung in the ignition. Almost gingerly he fired the engine, bracing even though it would do neither Cyria or Bordelon any good if—he pushed back explosive thoughts and gritted his teeth. If they didn't drive away, the outcome would not be better.

He put the car in gear, glancing once more at the door. The two men were still there. Was there movement behind the two? Was it a true sense that someone else was just out of sight watching them leave or paranoia? No, he trusted his gut, trusted the strong sense of being watched by hostile eyes. And woven through it was an uneasiness he couldn't understand. Bordelon, he thought, though it wasn't his gaze Archie sensed. His sense of unease spiked as the feeling of connection grew. Whoever it was, they knew each other.

His shoulders twitched, and he eased up on the brake so that the car started moving. The gates stood open, and he turned left at the street. He kept the speed down until they were out of sight of the mansion. Under the unease, urgency built. They needed to get clear of the car. No matter that it would be crazy for them to tamper with it—

First parking place he found, he pulled in. He didn't turn the engine off.

Laura opened her mouth, then closed it. Archie held a finger up to his lips as he eased his door open as quietly as he could. Laura did the same, leaving her door hanging open. Slow at first, then faster as the urgency built, he urged her as far from the car as their surroundings allowed. Standing half in front of her, he stared at the car, then looked down at Laura.

Her eyes were wide, her skin bleached of color.

"They wouldn't, would they?" she whispered.

Would they? He couldn't make a case for why, because it would be beyond stupid, but he felt it deep in his gut that someone wanted them—or him—dead and gone.

His mind ticked over, his certainty fading as nothing happened. He looked at his watch. How long had it been since he started the car? How far away would they want them to get— if they'd done something to the car? *If.*

It would be crazy, insane even. There were ways to find out where they'd been. Tracking data from their cell phones—

He froze and pulled his out. It was useless with the SIM card gone. But even that wouldn't solve their problem. He'd seen on a show where companies had tracking data from phones without cards and turned off. And he'd told Zach where they were. Cyria hadn't liked it much, but she hadn't objected.

"It's crazy…" Laura murmured, though without conviction.

He stared at the running car, half wondering why someone didn't try to steal it. He took a half step toward it. They could have tampered with the brakes. Or been tracking them. Listening and hoping to hear where the necklace was. Blowing them was the stupidest option. If they were listening in, well, they were having a good laugh right now. Because blowing it up would cause them more problems than not blowing them up? He repeated this in his head, but his gut remained unconvinced. If he looked at the underside of the car, would he know? There was the dash or under the seats—

"It's not my car," Laura said, half-despairing, half-hopeful. "If they do something to that car, Frank—"

Her words were cut off when flames ripped up through the front seats of the car. It lifted the center section up, then slammed it down, debris scattering out from it in all directions.

Archie had Laura down, his body over hers when the gas tank went up.

Muffled from under him and almost drowned out by the crackle of flames, Laura said, "I'm so toast."

"We will be if we don't get out of here," Archie said. He

helped her up, noted the incoming streetcar and said, "Let's catch that."

11
———

THEY SAT SIDE BY SIDE, not speaking as the streetcar lurched its way along St. Charles, taking them back toward Cyria's mansion, then past it. Laura had tensed and then found she couldn't relax even when nothing happened. She half shifted, opened her mouth, caught the curious gaze of the woman across from them, and pressed her lips back together. Laura waited until the woman noticed she was looking at her and then gave her a half smile that made her look away.

Archie didn't move when the car made the turn onto South Carrolton, or when it looped around for the trip back. Slowly, all the passengers with them left, replaced by new people. Laura usually liked people watching, but it was as if she were locked in a sort of bubble that separated her from everyone but Archie. She could see them, but was unable to process anything beyond the fact that some were women, some were men. She assumed it was shock, and possibly the remnants of what they'd used to drug her.

Someone drugged me.

When the car approached an intersection that was a short

walk to Zach's house, she made a half move. Archie's hand on her arm stopped her.

"Not yet."

She knew her eyes were big as she turned them on him.

"I need to think."

We can't ride the streetcar all day. She didn't say it out loud. He must have known that eventually, they would attract the attention of the driver—if they hadn't already.

As if that thought had occurred to Archie, too, he shifted, looping his arm over her shoulder and smiling down at her with his lips, while his eyes warned—or asked—her to play along. Because it was easier, she lowered her head to his shoulder, letting her hair fall forward to screen her face from watchers. This way Archie couldn't see her eyes, couldn't see her wanting it to be more than play...

For just a minute, she let herself listen to his heart beating, not thinking, just enjoying the feel of his arm around her. It would have been nice to stay in the moment, halted between where they'd been and where they needed to go, but out there somewhere...

"Zach won't just be worried," she murmured against his shoulder, his incredibly comforting shoulder. "If he hasn't already, he'll be baking the town with siblings and friends."

"I hope so," he murmured back. "It will make them harder to watch."

"But...why?" The word burst out, though she managed to keep the volume down. It was a relief to have the question out there, though. Even through the daze, through the shock, the "why" had repeated with each click of the streetcar's wheels as it rolled along the track. Why take the risk? What had they hoped to accomplish? What was worth getting the Bakers all stirred up? Their murder would only draw more attention to the beads and put them even more out of reach. And if they were a copy?

Again, what were they afraid of? And if what they feared was so bad, why let them leave the house? She'd read enough mysteries to know a few ways they could have made it look like they'd gone somewhere else and died there? Why wait? Why a bomb? Why? Why? Why?

The refrain was a wail inside her head, but she clamped her lips together, her hands curled into fists in her lap as if that would help her lips stay sealed shut.

Archie didn't answer, which was not a surprise. Where her head rested, he vibrated with tension. She could almost feel him thinking, straining to work it out. As if he sensed her own strain, the hand not resting on her shoulder settled on top of her fisted hands. Their warmth startled her. She did not know how she could be cold, for the day had turned warm, and the sun beat through the window next to her. Shock, she reminded herself. Shock and fear. Her lips might have twisted wryly as she thought about Frank. He loved that car. She hoped he loved her more and he probably did, but when he found out she wasn't dead, and his car was? She'd rather not be there for that moment.

After a time, the trolley stopped in front of Audubon Park. To her surprise, Archie rose, pulling her with him. They clambered down and crossed over into the park. People milled around, which was kind of comforting. A couple got up from a bench, and Archie snagged it for them, earning a few scowls, but the look he shot back had the bench hopefuls moving on.

The sun was starting down, extending the shadows of trees and people. In the summer, it would be hot, the air thick with the scent of flowers, grass, and leaves, but in January there was a tinge of rotting stuff in there. The light was thinner somehow, just a hint of the cooler air that would flow in when the sun ceased to rule the sky. The river was close enough for her to hear the boats calling out and there was the zoo. Could she hear the animals, or did she imagine their sounds because she knew the zoo was there?

The shock must be fading because the figures moving around her began to take on more definition than boy or girl. A gaggle of schoolgirls in their uniforms laughed shrilly as they passed by. Under a nearby tree, a young man lay on a blanket ,his attention on a thick book. On the next bench, a young mother tapped on her phone while her child—

Laura straightened with a jerk. "My purse—" And her phone.

Archie's arm came around her again. "It wouldn't have helped." He showed her his phone. "They took the SIM card out."

"You can get another SIM card," she pointed out. But her purse. It wasn't the perfect purse, but it had been filled with her things, some useful, others...well, they were dear. People probably didn't carry small snapshots anymore, but she'd had one of her with her mother. Was it irreplaceable? She didn't know. There were the discontinued lipstick and the little mirror that had been a gift from Nell when she married Alex. A sort of not bridesmaid's gift. A vintage box she'd found in the French Quarter that she used for Tylenol and ibuprofen. And of course, her credit cards, driver's license, and a small amount of cash. A very small amount.

And her cellphone. Did she even know her dad's number? Or Frank's? Who you gonna call when all your phone numbers just got blown to pieces? There might have been a bit of a whine to that question, but hadn't she earned a little whine-one-one after the day she'd had? A day that had started just after midnight, had been mostly sleepless and included a drugging and an explosion. And LaFon—

She pushed back against this thought. The weight of it was

too much to deal with right now. He was dead. She couldn't change that.

And she was alive. There was guilt, but also relief. She looked up. She could still see the sun. Could still inhale the slightly rancid air. Could still feel the brush of her shoulder against the guy who would leave if they continued to survive. Who would leave, she repeated firmly. Their current closeness was the result of the danger, not his choice. Or hers.

She added that last for her own pride. She would not be desperate, clingy, or needy even if she did have an almost over-whelming urge to suck her own thumb.

Archie, who had been staring at his phone during the whole of her mental whine, gave the phone a small shake, as if that would clear things up.

"Why?" He leaned back, shaking his head now. "It's like trying to see through a thick fog." His free hand lifted, reaching out. "I can feel it right there, but I can't see—"

When they were called to a scene, it could be like that. Most times the problem was pretty obvious, but not always. People took drugs or had health conditions they couldn't explain. All they could do was start with the basics. Take their life signs, look at their nails, their eyes—

"What can you see?" she asked. She half shifted so that she could see him, and told him what she'd just thought about taking life signs, then asked again, "What do you see?"

He started to shake his head, then sighed, doing his own shift, so he half faced her, resting his arm along the back of the bench, close but not quite touching her. He frowned, but it was a thinking frown, not an angry one.

"You don't just look," he muttered. "You listen, too."

"True." If she closed her eyes, shut out what she'd seen at Cyria's house, what would she hear? The creak of wood, the clink of dishes and her heels...the unsettling rumble from the gators...movement out in the hall. Cyria's voice sharp with—fear? She'd looked annoyed, Laura recalled, but the tone of her voice had been...afraid. Who had she been afraid they'd see? Or was afraid would see them? It wasn't Bordelon because he let them out of the bedroom.

"There was someone in the hall when we were outside," Archie said slowly.

"Someone who didn't want to be seen," Laura agreed, recalling the shadowy presence. "The person Cyria didn't want to come in while we had tea and drugs."

Archie's mouth twitched in a half smile, half grimace. "Yeah." He sighed. "I feel..."

"What?"

"A bit Obi-wan," he admitted, the smile winning against the grimace this time. "Like I sensed something from a long time ago."

"Something?" she prompted.

"Someone."

A long time ago was probably... "Seventeen years ago."

He shifted in the seat. "Maybe. Probably, but...why?"

"Maybe something seventeen years ago subconsciously bothered you, and it has surfaced now because of the beads." She hesitated. "Were you uneasy? Back then? You said you told him not to get involved with Auguste?"

"Yeah, but Auguste didn't hide from me. He wasn't thrilled to see me, but he wasn't worried either. Why would he—no." He shook his head sharply this time. "This is someone who does not want to be seen. Is willing to kill to not be seen." He looked at her now, his gaze haunted. "It's someone who knows me well enough to know I won't stop until I find out what happened."

She frowned. "Wouldn't that have to be someone pretty close to you?"

It was his turn to frown. "Rob didn't bring his friends around a lot after he started the business. He was busy."

There was a hint of defensiveness in the excuse. Laura opened her mouth and then closed it. If someone criticized one of her siblings—deserved or not—they closed ranks. It was clear that Archie had looked up to his big brother, possibly idolized him after he died.

"His family was young, too. A lot going on. Nothing that would have mattered if we'd known…"

Archie rubbed his face in frustration and Laura once more bit back a comment.

"But if it was someone who knew Rob. If he talked about us—"

One did, she knew. Idle chat. Maybe bragging about good news. Funny stories shared. Everyone did it. But this time—the lowering sun wasn't the only thing making tiny chills dance across her skin.

"A…friend?" Not a very good friend.

He looked at her without answering. He didn't have to. She could see it in his eyes.

"So the beads are probably…the same ones in the photo?" she said that instead of the other obvious: that Rob must have been murdered, had to have been killed for the beads to survive. Or they'd been switched before he walked into that tower. Betrayed or betrayer? It was not a question she could ask Archie. Had someone murdered Rob or gotten lucky? And if someone had, well, Hebert, their only link to that person, was dead, too. Cyria seemed to be trying to find out more, as well. Seemed to be, she reminded herself. She could have been trying to find out what they knew. But then she'd stopped. Had hardly asked anything. Drugged her and let them leave. Okay, there was the bomb. Had she ordered the bomb planted or had someone else done it while they were inside? The gate had been open, the car sitting out in plain view with the keys in the ignition. And if it had been someone else—why had she let them leave without asking much of anything? Her thoughts circled close, but she moved away, picking another question to obsess over.

Something had changed from when they'd been hijacked. Something? Or someone? What?

"Cyria didn't seem to know who you were..." she said slowly, knowing that could have been a ruse. But still, the drug had to have already been in Laura's cup. They knock her out and then what? Listen to her snore—if she believed her brothers which she totally didn't.

Unless—Laura slanted Archie a look, this time letting the question happen inside her head because if she kept avoiding it...

She mentally pressed on against the pain in her heart, not to mention a brain that wanted to vehemently reject it. What if they'd all talked while she was out? All. Including Archie. What if they planned. Conspired even. Archie saving her life could be part of it.

He'd managed to isolate her from her family. She was without money and phone, not to mention transportation. She was sitting in a public park that was fine at the moment, but as soon as the sun set...

All of her instincts said that Archie wasn't—that he wouldn't —but she wouldn't be the first woman fooled by a man able to hide who and what he really was.

Trust. It was only this moment, with her life on the line, that she realized how slippery trust was in concept. Trust could be given on consignment, as it were, with the understanding that over time it must be earned, or it would be withdrawn. Over time. She didn't have time. Indeed, the clock in her head seemed to tick louder and louder. While this was not her area of expertise, it was not entirely different from a medical emergency. As if she were assessing life signs, she felt the approach of the critical mass building, the sense that the wave was going to break whether she was ready or not. And a bunch of other metaphors she couldn't quite pull up. But lots of them. The moment was a metaphor-rich zone.

She stole another glance at Archie. The line of his mouth was grim, his brooding gaze fixed on a couple passing on the path in front of them. And then, as if time itself rippled, his head turned, his gaze meeting hers. Grim turned rueful, possibly a bit frustrated. He rubbed his hands across his head, ruffling his hair.

Did reason return or get sideswiped by the cute guy? Reason said Archie had no reason to conspire against her. She was a pawn, the temporary owner of some beads. She knew less than Sergeant Schultz from *Hogan's Heroes*. Which was less than nothing. Possibly in the black hole of negative. If Cyria and her friends had wanted to talk with Archie, they could have done it without her—sleeping or awake.

"We need to get out of sight before it gets dark. They can't watch everyone we know..." His voice trailed off.

Laura looked around her. They were about a fifteen-minute walk from Zach's house, possibly longer based on her current state of tired. Zach wasn't likely to be there—her heart constricted sharply at what she was putting him through. How long would it take for them to realize the car had been empty? Probably not as long as they'd been out wandering. Knowing she wasn't in that car wouldn't help completely, because hello, missing.

And Frank, she did not want to think about Frank or Frank's car. So, the house. It was the most obvious place to go, which meant it might be the safest place to go right now. Except for the beads. Had Zach taken them back to the house? She rubbed her aching head, wishing she could stop her brain from doing its gerbil on a wheel thing.

"I wish," His lips twisted. "I wish it had stayed buried."

She didn't have to ask what he meant.

"That we'd met without—" He stopped again, while a tiny curl of happy poked its head out of the mire inside her head. Did that mean he would have gone on the blind date anyway?

His hand lifted to push her hair back behind her ear. The arm along the back of the bench lightly stroked her shoulder. She felt it when his gaze found her mouth. Felt her lips soften and part slightly. The fingers brushing her cheek trembled a bit.

"Laura..." The word was more a sigh of regret, so she was not surprised when he said, "I wish—I'm not the marrying kind."

She gave a choked half laugh. "I think what you aren't is the stay married kind."

This startled a laugh out of him. Then his chest moved in a deep sigh. "I wonder...

His hands still lightly touched her, but she felt him move back. And she sensed the ghost of his dead brother reforming between them.

She couldn't explain why this tilted the trust deck in his direction, just knew that it had.

Her lips might have trembled, but she firmed them up and threw some stiffening into her back.

"Zach's house is not that far away. We can walk there—" She held up a hand as he started to protest. "Do you really think I don't know a back way in?"

12

LAURA COULD HAVE BEEN LEADING Archie anywhere, but since she seemed to know where she was going, he kept pace with her while keeping an eye on their surroundings—and the rapidly setting sun. He did not want them to be out on the street in the dark. Laura seemed to share his desire because she kept the pace brisk. Just when he started to question his own fitness regime, she slowed, only now taking a good look around before leading him down a track that appeared to cut through a block of houses.

When he was totally turned around, she stopped again.

"Can you jump it, or do we risk the gate?"

Since she already had her hand on the metal fence and her knees partly bent, his pride told her, "Jump."

She went over lightly, landing like a gymnast on the other side. He was just glad he made it to the other side and didn't fall on his face.

"Stick close to me," she whispered.

It wasn't a painful request, and it was a good plan since there were patches of shade that could have tripping risks.

"Aren't you a bit old to be sneaking in?" an old, amused but low voice asked from a window that he realized was open.

"It's complicated, Miss Josephine," Laura whispered back.

"It always is." There was a pause. "Better take this."

Something long and thin extended out the window, the end held by a wrinkled claw.

Laura took it, hefting it in her hand. "Nice bat. Didn't we—"

"I wouldn't go there, dear," the sweet, old voice advised. "Probably need this, too."

This time it was a rolling pin. Laura passed him the bat and took this. She appeared to hesitate, though he couldn't be sure. As if the old lady knew what they needed to know, she spoke.

"Someone's already rooting around in there. Again."

This time Laura looked back at him, her eyes wide in the near dark.

"Really." Laura sounded more thoughtful than worried. "Have you—of course you have. How long do we have before the cops arrive?"

"Just got off the phone," the old lady said. "Time for this I suppose."

The claw came out again. Archie couldn't see what she gave Laura this time.

"Did I ever tell you—" Laura began.

"That I'm the best ever," the old lady finished. "Lost count, dear. Rather you found me a man."

"I'll see what I can do," Laura promised.

"Suppose that one's taken?"

Archie felt his cheeks heat and tried to remember the last time that had happened.

"Divorced twice," Laura pointed out.

"I can work with that." The old lady's chuckle was soft and a bit evil.

Archie was not sorry when Laura moved forward again,

though he couldn't resist a look in the window. All he could see was two circles with violet irises. He blew her a kiss and once past her window, paused when Laura did.

"Here."

The object was warm and round and— "A cookie?"

"Try it," Laura suggested.

Archie did. "If we survive, I might just go back and ask her to be the third Mrs. Gunn."

"You'd be her fifth, or that might be the sixth. The woman can cook." The shadow had eased enough for him to see the soft curve of her mouth before she popped the last of the cookie into her mouth. She chewed and swallowed then said, "I feel better."

Strangely enough, so did he.

————

Laura slowed their progress even more as she tried to pierce the darker spots. She wasn't as familiar with Zach's strip of backyard as she used to be. A stand of trees mostly blocked the back of the house, but through the one visible window, she saw flashes of light moving around, some bouncing off the trees. Someone was in there and that someone was using a flashlight, she guessed. Since the porch light had come on, it wasn't because of a power outage.

"How long do you think we have?" Archie whispered, the words tickling against her ear because he'd leaned in so close.

"Five, maybe ten minutes." It all depended on where the Bakers were clustered at the moment. If she had to make a wild guess, she'd put them all at the St. Charles house of Nell's friend, Sarah. It was the only place big enough to hold them all plus any extras. And Sarah ran a catering business, so the odds of there being food being available was higher there. The Bakers knew better than to let stress and worry stop them from eating.

She hoped they were there because Sarah was probably the only one who could talk Frank down off the roof about his car when he found out it had blown up.

She took Archie's hand and led him toward the right, away from the driveway and the back door. The house had three bedrooms: the girls' room, the boys' room, and Zach's room. The kids' rooms each had an, um, damaged screen and a window latch that could be jiggered from the outside if one knew the trick of it—which she did. Since any egress and entry woke up any siblings currently occupying either room, they weren't as useful as they could have been until the sibling levels thinned. The boys' room was easier to get into because the big A/C unit was right outside their window. The fact that it didn't work half the time was irrelevant when effecting entry. It was the one most used because the boys had left home first. If any of the girls had hoped Zach would turn it into a single, those hopes had been dashed. He'd just divided them in half, perhaps hoping that the girls would be a check on each other.

As she eased up to what was still known as the boys' room, she realized whoever had gotten in had already used this window. The screen was on the ground, the window hanging wide. They could wait here, hoping the perp or perps came back this way, but it would be faster for them to run out the back door if they got interrupted—or if they found what they were looking for.

She shifted around the side of the house, closing on the girls' room. No signs of entry here. Her only fear was that the long lack of use would make it noisy to try.

Archie touched her shoulder, then handed her a pocket knife, handle in her direction, and one of the blades already extended. She gave him the rolling pin and went to work, aware of the clock ticking down to the arrival of the police. She got the screen free without a squeak. Her sisters always said she had the best hands. She applied the knife in the right spot and added some careful pressure. There was a small click when the latch gave. She froze, but there was no sign of awareness from inside the house as the window swung slowly wide.

With it open, they could now hear muffled sounds of movement. She leaned close to Archie's ear. "Bedroom door should still be closed." Not even flashes were cutting the dark, so this seemed like a good intel. "It squeaks at five o'clock." She added a quick layout of the room and what lay beyond.

He nodded, handed her the rolling pin and took the knife back. She didn't see what he did with it but accepted the bat from him, too. Despite his somewhat clumsy leap over the fence, the window didn't seem to pose any difficulty for him. He hoisted himself soundlessly up and in. She handed him both of Miss Josephine's weapons, then accepted his help getting inside. She might be surprised he didn't want her to stay outside.

The bedroom used to be more crowded since they'd needed three bunk beds back in the day. Now it had her bedroom furniture dotted around it. Once inside, she led Archie to the door and eased it open—stopping just before the five o'clock squeak.

"Wait here," he ordered.

The words were so soft, she wasn't sure she heard them. She considered them and mostly agreed with him. Even with a rolling pin, she didn't think she'd be much use. Despite this, she ghosted out the door. It was only a couple of steps across the hall to the boys' room. This door was open. She didn't touch it. Knew how to avoid any boards that creaked as she positioned herself behind the door. The least she could do was cut off this retreat if someone did come back this way. Did she feel guilty that she didn't expect this to happen? A little. Mostly she felt relieved. She wasn't sure she could whack someone on the head with a rolling pin.

Archie was glad he'd been in the house when the lights were on. Laura's quick summary might not have been enough otherwise. He was also helped some by the intruder's flashlight as whoever held it moved around. Based on what could be seen from the light that came in from the street, he'd already been through the living room. Now he was in the kitchen.

That was good. And bad.

Archie was familiar with the kitchen, but it had that back door close by for a quick exit. On the possible upside, that was also the direction the police would come. As near as he could tell, no one used the front door of this house. It was possible it had forgotten how to open.

He eased down the hall, carefully checking each board before putting his weight on it. Outside, the lights of a passing car made the dimly seen figure tense. It shifted giving Archie a glimpse of light on metal.

A gun. Of course, the guy had a gun. He didn't feel a chauvinist for expecting a guy, and he was pretty sure he knew who it was.

"It's got to be here."

Archie tensed. Yup. It was Bordelon but why—

Someone out of sight grunted. Crap. There were two of them. Archie had that frisson down the back feeling without knowing why, and not just because the odds got slightly worse for him. But then, ever since he got to New Orleans, he'd been feeling off for some reason, more so since the hijacking. That old, far off feeling of recognition. His lips twisted. He needed an Obi-wan. He shoved the feeling to one side.

He hoped Laura had done what he asked her and stayed put.

A glass fell to the floor. Bordelon cursed as his feet crunched over it. Archie used the noise to move closer.

And then Archie heard the distant sound of sirens.

Time's up, he thought and launched himself on Bordelon.

They both went down with a crash, a wild roll that slammed Archie into table and chair legs, tumbling with at least one chair on top of them. Later it would hurt but adrenalin drove him now, one arm locked around Bordelon and the other around the wrist of the hand with the gun.

He was aware of a figure moving to stand over them. He kicked out with a leg and the figure staggered. Metal gleamed in the dark figure's hand. Archie rolled Bordelon on top and tried to turn his gun toward the figure.

The silence was unsettling, and that feeling grew. *I know this guy.*

He tightened his hold on Bordelon, but the guy was a street fighter. They rolled until he was on top again.

"Shoot him," Bordelon grunted.

Archie almost didn't hear the click. With a superhuman heave, he managed to get Bordelon between them again. In his mind's eye, it felt like he could see the guy trying to get a bead on him. Or decide to shoot them both?

He heaved Bordelon up and off him. Heard a muffled curse and light flashed. Bordelon gave a pained grunt.

"Bastard—"

Archie rolled into a shadow, reaching for his pocketknife, but the footsteps pounded down the hall away from him.

In Laura's direction.

He scrambled up, but Bordelon—wounded but still capable of a fight—tackled him.

He brought his knee up, felt breath leave Bordelon's body. He had a moment before Bordelon recovered, and he used it with punishing force. Bordelon went limp, dazed or out cold. Archie didn't care.

He scrambled up and ran down the hall. The silence

brought his heart up into his throat. If something had happened to her—

The back door rattled, and voices called out the usual cop warning, but he ignored them, too. Sounds of a scuffle had him speeding up. The thud against wood happened just as he made a sliding stop and almost didn't make the turn into the room. His foot caught on something, and he staggered but managed to stay upright.

"Laura!" The panic in his voice made him wince.

"I'm all right." Her voice sounded shaky. "I...hit him. I wasn't sure I could, but I did." She sounded surprised.

"Good thing," he said, wrapping her in his arms. "Where's the light switch."

"Right behind you."

He groped and found it, flipped it on. Winced as the light hit his pupils. When they'd shrunk down enough, he looked down. Laura was lucky. The guy was big—something about him made his heartbeat pick up. He was dressed all in black and had his head and face covered. The gun lay close to his slack hand.

Archie put Laura to the side and kicked the weapon aside— no way he'd pick it up with the cops kicking the door in—and then knelt by the slack figure and heaved him over onto his back. For half a second he hesitated, then ripped the mask off.

His world crashed, harder than it had on nine eleven.

As if she sensed something, Laura crouched next to him. "Archie, what's wrong? Who is that?"

"Rob. It's...Rob." The flatness of his voice surprised him. Inside his head, as if on a loop, he heard his mother sobbing when she'd realized her firstborn son was gone.

"Your brother?"

"No." He took a breath as Rob's eyes flickered, then opened. Archie felt his body harden. "He's not my brother."

13

AT SOME POINT, someone had wrapped a blanket around Laura where she sat on the edge of her bed. She had a vague memory of one of the beat cops guiding her out of the room, past Archie, past—her mind flinched away, and she shivered, pulling the blanket tighter. No one had asked her who was legit and who wasn't. They knew her. Knew Zach. Archie—her brain flinched again. Her last sight of him, they'd been giving him a wide berth, too. His eyes...

Her sisters were there with her, Hannah and Ingrid on either side patting her back and sometimes her clenched hands, the rest perched on what they could find around her. No one spoke. No one asked her how she was. They knew something was wrong. She was pretty sure they didn't know what—

She stared at the floor so she didn't have to see...him...Rob... taken out in handcuffs. Not looking didn't help. Her mind still played the scene over and over. She didn't have to see him taken out to see it. She didn't have to see Archie because she'd already seen his eyes. She could feel his pain from here.

She wished she had the right to hold him, the way her sisters held her. She was wounded because he was suffering. Her pain was his. But she didn't have the right to comfort him. She didn't have the right to feel this way. She couldn't help it, couldn't stop it, so she stared at the floor and wished...

There was a stir in the doorway. A throat cleared. She lifted her lids. Frank. Great. His gaze, above a wry twist of lips, was worried.

"Remind me not to trade cars with you again."

The words fell into the room and died a quick death. He shifted, looked around for a place to sit. There wasn't one.

"Gunn...Archie isn't saying anything. Can you—they need to talk to you."

She lifted her chin. It was something she could do for him. "Of course." She glanced around. "Where—"

"Here." His chin jerked. "Everyone out but Laura."

There was a general shuffle as her sisters left, probably adding to the overcrowding of an already crowded crime scene in the kitchen. The hall cleared for a moment, and Laura saw Becca. She paused, her eyes haunted, then she passed into Zach's bedroom. Was Archie still in there? She felt a stab in her chest. She was glad Becca was there for him. Really she was. A form blocked the doorway.

Laura straightened and pushed the blanket back. She dug around until she found EMT Laura deep inside her head. When she was pretty sure her outside was aligned with her inside she looked up. It was Logan Ferris. Odd that it felt both easier and harder for it to be him, but better than getting Alex.

"Hey, Laura." He sat down next to her.

"Logan." Her voice sounded calmer than she expected. It helped. "What do you need to know?"

"We need to know what happened."

Of course, they did. So they'd know who to arrest.

She nodded, mentally arranging the pieces in a line in front of her. "We drove to Archie's..." It amazed her that her voice didn't shake when she said Archie's name, "hotel and then..."

———

Archie felt the bed depress and saw Becca out of the corner of his eye. He didn't speak, but she wasn't his mom's friend for nothing. She took his hand, clasping it between both of hers.

"I don't know what happened here, Archie, and I wish, well, I wish your mom was here—"

The sharp movement was not something he could control. "No." The single word was a dry rasp of sound. He couldn't see his mom's face, couldn't see anything but Rob's eyes—but somehow not Rob's eyes—staring at him. Not sorry. Not ashamed. His brother but not his brother. A stranger in Rob's body.

A stranger who had tried to hide, to kill? His mind flinched at the word and he made himself think it. Rob had tried to kill him, to kill Laura. That's why he'd felt something at Cyria's house. He'd sensed this familiar stranger that used to be the best—

His thoughts fractured. He felt his grip tighten on Becca's. She might have winced.

"Sorry," he muttered, forcibly straightening the fingers.

"How can I help, Archie?" Gentle fingers smoothed the hair back from his face.

She couldn't help. No one—and from the rubble inside his head, he realized one person—could. One person had.

Laura.

He wanted to wrap his arms around her and cry like he had the day Rob died—the day he thought Rob died.

"How...how is Laura?" It amazed him he got the question out

with a voice that was stiff, but it didn't tremble. Inside...there was a lot of tremble.

"She's worried about you," Becca said.

That yanked his chin up. He stared at her. "Worried? About me?" Was she? A sliver of warm drifted up from the place where he used to have a heart...

"I'm..." He couldn't say it without a couple of tries. "Fine. I'm fine."

She squeezed his hand again. "This is bigger than a brawl, more than an interrupted break-in."

Archie sensed someone was there, in the doorway and looked up. Zach. Great. But his eyes weren't glaring. He wasn't showing much love, but no hate. Yet. He stiffened when Zach left the doorway and sat down on Archie's other side. For a moment, his hand hovered, and then Zach dropped it on his own knee and not Archie's.

"I'm sorry, son."

Archie didn't know why shame surged up inside. He wasn't the one who—

He stared at the closet door in front of him. "Laura told you."

"She told Ferris as part of her witness statement," Zach corrected. "I might have listened in."

Archie turned to stare—or possibly glare—at him.

"It had to be said, son."

It had to be said. Zach was right. It needed to be said. He needed to say it.

"My brother isn't dead. Rob isn't dead. He's not—" The hero Archie imagined, the big brother who he'd pictured trying to save those around him and losing his life. He wasn't dead. He hadn't saved anyone but himself. He was the bad guy. "He's not my brother," he repeated. "Maybe he never was."

He heard a sound and looked up. Laura stood in the hall

outside this room. Her lips moved. Maybe they trembled. He didn't know. He stared at her, wishing—

She came toward him, slowly, as if giving him the chance to tell her to go. He felt the bed move as first Becca, then Zach rose. Laura walked up to him. His arms closed around her middle, almost convulsively. He leaned in until his head rested against her, her heart beating against the side of his face. One of her arms looped around him, held him close and the other hand began to stroke the back of his head. She didn't speak. She didn't tell him it would be all right. She didn't tell him he would get over it.

She just held him. Through the tangle of pain, he felt something else from her.

Love.

It was selfish. He was an even worse mess than the last two times he'd tried love. But he leaned in and let it wash over him. Let it be the balm for his wounds...

14

"NIGHT, TASH." Laura gave her new partner a weary smile and climbed out of their rig. They'd been riding together for a week now, were starting to get comfortable with each other, learning to know and anticipate each other's moves. She'd been grateful to get back to work, thankful for long hours with blaring sirens and flashing lights because they kept her mind off Archie, who had flown home to tell his parents about Rob. She wished she could work twenty-four hours a day until she couldn't think or feel.

She wasn't sleeping anyway. She knew the family was building toward an intervention. Somehow all of her sisters had managed to stop by and give her the side eye. A couple of the brothers had stopped by, too, but they'd managed to avoid all eye contact.

So typical.

Their visits were easier, though. No one could accuse any of her brothers of being overly bright and perky. Okay, her sisters weren't either, but they talked. Mostly they talked around Laura's elephant, but she could tell they were edging closer. Her problem was she had nothing to tell them.

She and Archie weren't an item, they weren't even an item-in-embryo. They were two ships who'd crashed in the night. And Archie's ship wasn't the stay-married kind, so it had sailed away.

She stared in the mirror, remembering the night she'd been given the beads. It felt like years since That Night. Or That Weekend. She still hadn't added up the hours to know which it was. Perhaps the Never-Ending Not-Date was a better description.

She knew more than she had a month ago.

She knew her feelings for Archie had gone deeper than she wanted or planned. She refused to use the "l" word, but it was circling out there like her sisters. She was not going to let it land, because what was the point? Archie was gone. He'd be back to testify if it came to a trial. It was possible he'd come back with his parents. They were angry, at least Zach said they would be, but they'd still want to see the son they thought they'd lost.

They wouldn't find him, at least, she didn't think so, based on what she saw that night. Whatever path Rob had trod the last seventeen years, it had hardened him, killed what light he'd had before.

Details had come out. From Frank. Yeah, they should have asked Frank, but they hadn't.

No one, not even Frank, was saying it where it could be written down, but the general feeling was that Rob had been turned by Cyria, i.e., seduced. At least someone had seduced someone. They may have hastened her husband's demise and had been a version of a couple for a long time. Once the legal hounds started looking, there were pictures of the couple together, an evidence trail to follow to a pretty ugly place.

Bordelon, or Baby Bacchus Bordelon if one wanted to use his legal name, had been denied bail when traces of Hebert's and LaFon's blood had been found on his car. And matching traces of paint had been removed from both bodies. The theory was that Hebert had stolen the beads and they'd killed LaFon because they thought he knew something.

It looked like justice would happen. It wasn't enough, but it was something.

Cyria was tangled in the mess, too, when Archie's friend matched the green goo taken off Hebert to the green goo from her alligator pond. Even Auguste was having problems as Cyria, Baby Bordelon, and Rob turned on each other.

So much for true love, she thought, as she headed out to the curb to wait for Frank to pick her up. He was driving her car again, until the insurance got worked out for his. But it wasn't Frank waiting outside. She knew it even though all she could see was an outline of someone leaning against the side of a car.

Not her car. Not her brother.

Archie.

He straightened as she approached, his hands shoved into his pant's pockets.

"Hi."

"Hi." Brilliant, Laura. Questions tumbled in her head, but none of them wanted to come out her mouth. She and her questions were chickens. "You're back."

Oh, even better. Don't know what to say so state the obvious.

Even with the streetlights trying to help her out, she couldn't see enough to read his expression. And what the light did show, there wasn't much there anyway. The guy had a serious poker face.

"Yeah." He ran a hand over the top of his head. "My parents wanted to see Rob."

His voice was so neutral it hurt.

Becca had told her there was also a wife and kids.

As if he heard her, he added, "Hailey, Rob's wife, is trying to figure out how you divorce someone who was declared legally dead." He hesitated. "She didn't want to tell the kids, but the story is spreading. I think they took it better than she did."

"I can't imagine..." Her voice trailed off. She couldn't imagine how Hailey felt, but she'd seen Archie's eyes, had felt his pain like a current when she'd held him that night, had stayed with him until her legs almost gave way. It was Becca who finally came in. Archie had pulled away and, until this moment, hadn't looked back as far as she could tell.

He pulled open the car door and arched his one brow. She hesitated, but what would she gain by making him ask? And it was obvious Frank wasn't coming. Which was...interesting, now that she thought about it. What had Archie said to him? How did men manage to communicate when they appeared to say so little?

She slid in. Archie shut the door, and then walked around, and slid in beside her. He put the key in the ignition but didn't start the car. Oddly enough, the silence wasn't uncomfortable, at least for Laura. Despite her best efforts, there was a little tremor of happy trying to get some traction in the area of her heart. It was...good...to see him.

"Do...they want to see him?" she asked. "His kids."

"No." His hands clenched on the steering wheel. "He did agree to see my parents but..."

She would never forget Rob's eyes. So bitter. So devoid of emotion. Not even a twinge of shame at being caught. He'd chosen a good partner in Bordelon. They were both dead souls. Before she could stop herself, she covered the hand she could reach with one of hers. "They lost him again." *You all lost him again.*

"Yeah." He looked down, his lips twisted, then he gave a mighty sigh and tried to shrug it off. "It..."

"Sucks..." Laura supplied.

He gave a ghost of a grin. "Yeah." He reached to put the car in gear, then stopped again. "Nothing like having the scales ripped off your eyes to realize..."

He stopped gazing straight ahead, then he looked at her, and the expression, the change in them made her catch her breath.

"Rob's been a shadow over me for too long. I can't, I don't blame him for my two failed marriages, but, well, my second ex told me that he was the ghost between us. I didn't understand then. I do now. I don't...I'm done letting a ghost live in my head. It's going to take time, but I realized something while I was gone."

He shifted to face her, changing so that he gripped her hand now.

"What was that?" she asked, her voice a choked whisper. Because what she saw in his face, in his eyes sent her heart into overdrive with hope.

"That night, when you held me," he looked down and took a couple of breaths, then looked at her again, "when you held me, there was no ghost. There was just me and you. And there was," he sighed again, "light in the dark."

He lifted her hand to his mouth, watching to see if she objected, then pressed his lips to the back.

Maybe it was because she was super tired and hallucinating, but it seemed as if light spread down her arm and filled her, then flowed back to him. It didn't—it couldn't erase all the shadows in there, but it helped. It was a start. Perhaps, if he'd let her, they could push them all the way back. And turn him into not just the marrying kind, but the stay-married kind.

She waited, wondering if this was a thank you and goodbye or...

"Will you, is there room for a messed-up cop—"

She knew it, and then, oh crap. Another cop?

"In your life?"

She swallowed and found that instead of "are you kidding me?" what came out was, "I'd like that."

So gently, that tears pooled at the edges of her eyes, he eased her closer. He smoothed the hair back from her face with a hand that trembled, and when he lowered his mouth to hers, his gaze held hers until contact. His warm, gentle, and hot gaze trapped her in place as her lips quivered with anticipation. And as her lids slid down she saw not darkness, but light. Felt both desperation and hope in a kiss that was achingly gentle, that asked without taking.

Of course, her lips said yes. She loved this man. There, she'd admitted it. He was perfect for her.

And the chagrin of her seven brothers? It would be epic. They hadn't seen Archie coming. And it was way too late to run him off. Not only had she won, but she would give hope to her sisters.

Then the kiss ramped up and took her away. When it ended, she was breathless and happy, and fizzing inside like a firecracker. She rested her head on his shoulder, still amazed it was there and close and hers. Well, almost hers, she amended.

"Is it too soon to tell you I love you?" he asked.

She lifted her head and smiled. "It's exactly the right time to say it because I love you, too."

They'd said it. The "l" word, and the world hadn't stopped turning. Okay, so it had seen and heard it before, but never like this, like them. Stupid world, she thought, as his head lowered toward hers again...

———

Thank you for reading *Worry Beads!* I hope you enjoyed it. The next book in the series is *Fais Do Do Die!*

To find out about all my releases, be sure to sign up for my New Release eZine and get a free eBook by visiting my website..

If you enjoyed this book, I hope you'll consider leaving a review. It's not just because I'm needy (even though I try not to be!). Reviews help other readers decide which books to buy. :-)

FROM DO WAH DIDDY DIE

For more New Orleans fun, try *Do Wah Diddy Die:*

———

Luci Seymour - sexy & free spirited - returns to steamy New Orleans in search of the father she's never met. She finds murder, mayhem, love and adventure when her timing puts her directly in the sights of an elderly hit couple and a con man's last scam.

———

Mickey Ross was not a happy man.

He'd just come off a two-day stakeout and had the rumpled suit and unshaven chin to prove it. He was tired. He was cranky. And he wasn't home in bed having that dream where the cover girl for Sports Illustrated was rubbing sun tan lotion onto his back.

He looked at where he didn't want to be, but the waiting area of the New Orleans International Airport didn't fade to something more pleasing. Nor did the stuffed pig dangling at the end of his arm vanish into the nightmare realm where it belonged.

Mickey glared down at it. Bad enough for a cop to be keeping company with any pig, but this pig, well, if it's lurid pink and purple surface was any indication, it had never been a beauty. Time had rubbed away the fluff from its surface and left one sorry black eye hanging by a single thread over the patchy remains of a black grin on its square snout. Its tattered ensemble began and ended with a limp ribbon knotted around a fat neck.

In an effort to distance himself from his ratty companion, Mickey held it by the tatty end of the ribbon and twirled it with more than a hint of vindictiveness.

In between twirls, he pondered the unkind fate that had landed him in this fix. If Eddie hadn't decided to end sixty years of bachelorhood, he wouldn't be waiting for a damn flower girl for the damn wedding, with only a stuffed pig for an introduction. Who flew in a little girl for a geriatric wedding anyway? New Orleans was full of little girls who'd probably love tossing petals. But no, they had to import one, then pick a total stranger to collect her—with an obnoxious pig as the icebreaker. Convenient that Eddie had discovered pressing business in Mandeville tonight.

The least he could have done was warn him about the old ladies. How could his own uncle send him into battle, into that minefield of weirdness, without even a warning? A minefield that had kept going off in his face no matter what he did, a horror—except for the one small oasis of sanity known as Miss Gracie, who had saved him from the stuffed dragon, but not the pig.

He just wished he knew where Eddie's Unabelle—was that a name to make a guy flinch—fit in with the Seymour's. She didn't seem to be a relative. She was just...there, like a black hole. He sure hoped the lights were on in her upper story for Eddie or he'd learn there were worse things than a lonely retirement.

A stir at the gate quickly became arrival as passengers filtered off the plane. With the end in sight, Mickey straightened in hope.

That's when it occurred to his weary brain that a stuffed pig might be a less than adequate introduction to the kid. What had possessed the parents to entrust their kid to the uncertain care of three batty old ladies? He studied each small, whining arrival, wondering which one was his. A security guard loomed up on one side and he had to produce his badge.

The case against Eddie just kept building.

A woman emerged from the breezeway and paused to get her bearings. Mickey straightened in an utter and complete moment-of-silence respect for the best legs he'd ever been privileged to lay eyes upon. The cop part of him was vaguely aware she was in her late twenties, maybe early thirties, almost of a height with him and the possessor of a slender build. Her hair was dark and cut short around a face made interesting by its square jaw and straight, dark brows. Mouth was nice, too. Full and lush and lined in red.

He left off admiring her legs to contemplate her mouth, but his attention was drawn lower again when the legs went into motion. Brief appearances by her thighs, between the slash of her dark skirt, had him tugging at a too-tight tie. It took him a few seconds to realize that she'd stopped right in front of him.

With extreme reluctance, he dragged his gaze back to eye level. Her head was angled, her gaze directed toward the pig with a seriousness it didn't deserve. Just for a moment, something in the angle of her jaw had him wondering if he'd met her, but he dismissed the notion. A guy couldn't forget those legs.

His gaze drifted down again, but he flashed back to attention when she stepped closer, her nose bare inches from his, her lashes lifting with lust-building slowness to reveal emerald green depths.

His tie tightened to near strangulation level, but he couldn't move, let alone do something about it. Green eyes were always trouble for him. Too bad proximity and hormones took the edge off caution. If his partner, Delaney, were here, he'd recognize the signs of Mickey on the verge of falling in lust again. But Delaney wasn't here. The lucky bastard was in bed.

Carpe Diem. Mickey knew his smile was his best opening gambit and produced it with practiced ease. "Hello."

———

Luci studied the smile, recognized the confidence and the intent behind it. She'd met smiles like this one. Smiles that were confident of their charm. Smiles that expected weak knees and a cessation of rational thought. It was fortunate she had a built-in immune system to charming smiles and didn't ever do rational thought. It went with being a Seymour, though her knees, just for a moment, signaled a willingness to depart from the norm. She reminded herself she was the result of a departure from the norm and said, "That's my pig."

———

"When it comes to creating stories with offbeat humor and outrageous situations, Pauline Baird Jones is in a class by herself. A most excellent experience!" *RT Book Reviews*

To buy this book, click here.

FROM OPEN WITH CARE

Christmas has never been so....green...

———

The drive to crazy town was a good distraction from the Thing that Virginia Prescott did not want to think about. It helped that she needed to focus on the snowy, winding road in steadily worsening weather.

And if that didn't keep her mind off the Thing, there were her passengers.

It was probably her imagination that inimical gazes bored holes into her back. Gini risked a look in the rear view mirror and caught Isaac looking at her. He met her gaze for a second that felt longer than that, then it slid away with more composure than Gini had had at nine. Her twin sister's new stepson was a little scary.

Gini was still trying to figure out how Isaac and his sister had landed in the rear seat of her rented SUV. There were unmistakable signs they were not willing passengers for this trip. Isaac wasn't openly hostile—yet—but Daphne had made it clear Gini would have to bust an impossible move to rise to the level of pond scum.

Gini didn't blame them. They'd had no say in the very recent marriage of their dad, and it was clear that their absent-minded-professor-ish parent had either forgotten to brief them, or punted that job to her. Bif and Vanessa both worked at NASA, in the same department. It was how they met. But Gini didn't entirely buy into the "emergency" that had left her holding the kids. Not that she begrudged the newlyweds some alone time, but they'd better show up for Christmas. Or sooner. Both of them. Period.

The snow was showing up. From what she could see in the headlights, it was going to be a very white Christmas. It occasionally snowed in Dallas, but for the whitest of white holidays, she'd always had to come home. The swirling flakes had looked pretty dancing around the deer antler arch at the edge of the small Wyoming town where she and Van had grown up. The sight of it stirred her happy memory cortex. Would Van make it in time to watch *White Christmas* with them? Even if they didn't sing the "Sisters" song out loud—which would probably be an even worse sin than Van marrying the kids' dad—they'd exchange a look that said they were singing inside their heads. It was their song. And in the morning, after the presents and the feast—which could be great or awful depending how much access mom gave them to the kitchen this year—there'd be deep, white drifts for snowball fights and snow angels and sledding and getting so cold hot chocolate was necessary for survival—

As if Daphne sensed her happy thoughts and deplored them, Gini heard a sigh—and possibly felt it ruffle her hair—from the teen's side of the vehicle. It had a glare attached that drilled her between the shoulder blades. Sucked to be thirteen. And the two kids lived with their mom, so their dad not showing up at the airport to collect them would have upped the disappointment factor by an equation only Van was smart enough to figure out.

Gini had tried to lighten the atmosphere with some carols—the only music the radio could pick up—but that just seemed to expand the cloud of 'not happy' to the point of stifling, despite the headphones firmly clamped over Daphne's ears. She couldn't remember exactly how it felt to be thirteen, but she did remember not liking much, including herself. In distant memory of that awful time, Gini turned the happy—and the music—off. It was the least she could do. Possibly the only thing she could do.

Isaac also wore headphones. His game gave off an eerie green glow, like they were in a war bunker or something.

Ho, ho, ho.

She was kind of surprised that Grif hadn't responded to her text that she'd collected his children from the Cody airport. She'd even left off the guilt attachment, which was hugely magnanimous of her in her opinion. It was possible her timing was awkward. Or maybe there really was an emergency, though she couldn't imagine what emergency NASA could have. Daphne for sure hadn't believed it, if her extreme eye roll was any indication. Discontent was an almost visible haze back there, though it did go with the green glow.

She saw a familiar half rock, half log gate and took the turn. Almost there now. She kinda felt like she ought to warn them that there might be worse than an unwanted step aunt to face at the cabin, but she didn't know what version of crazy she'd find. Her mom, who had given birth very late in life, had been a solid twelve on a ten point weird scale—with ten being the most extreme—even before age had started to degrade her synapses. At least the incoming quirky-to-bat-crap-crazy-weird was a great distraction from—but she wasn't thinking about the Thing.

Her SUV swept around a corner and the edge of the lights

caught a blur of movement. Gini didn't hit the brakes, but she did take her foot off the gas. The thickening swirl of flakes remained mercifully clear of solid objects. She did not need to slam her rental into a deer. Not that—but the light and night must be playing tricks on her. She thought she'd seen a glimpse of a green little—but that was crazy, even for crazy town.

She'd checked the weather about a hundred times before boarding her plane, but the storm had stubbornly refused to commit until she was on the ground and headed for the cabin— a cabin her mom should *so* not be occupying, with or without a live-in care giver. And yet here Gini was, ferrying the reluctant step-grand kids over the frozen crick and through the snowy woods to step-grandma's house. She just prayed that Van and Grif would make it before the storm closed the road.

The eerie glow on Isaac's side of the car faded to black. For no reason she could identify, that made her uneasy.

———

If you like offbeat humor and outrageous situations, you'll love *Open With Care!*

ALSO BY PAULINE BAIRD JONES

Available in print, digital and audio.

Romantic Suspense

The Big Uneasy Series:

Relatively Risky (1)

Family Treed (A Big Uneasy Short Story)

Dead Spaces (2.0)

Louisiana Lagniappe (3.0)

Worry Beads (4.0)

Fais Do Do Die (5.0)

The Big Uneasy Bundle

Lonesome Lawmen Series:

The Last Enemy

Byte Me

Missing You

Lonesome Mama (Bonus short story)

(The *Lonesome Lawmen* is also available as a digital bundle)

Do Wah Diddy Die

The Spy Who Kissed Me

*Perilously Fun Fiction Bundle (*includes *The Spy Who Kissed Me* and *Do Wah Diddy Die.* Bonus: *Do Wah Diddy Delete Short Story Collection)*

Dangerous Dance

A Dangerous Duet - 2020

Science Fiction Romance/Paranormal

Project Universe Series:

The Key (book 1)

Girl Gone Nova (book 2)

Tangled in Time (book 3)

Steamrolled (book 4)

Kicking Ashe (book 5)

Found Girl (book 6)

Lost Valyr (book 7)

Maestra Rising (book 8)

Project Enterprise: The Short Stories

Time Trap: A Project Enterprise Series Short Story

The Real Dragon

Operation Ark: A Project Enterprise Story

Nebula Nine (time travel adventure)

Open With Care (Christmas collection that includes, "Riding For Christmas" and "Up on the House Top"

Specters in the Storm: A paranormal/steampunk/science fiction romance novella

Out of Time (World War II Time Travel Romance)

Just in Time (An Out of Time Adventure)

An Uneasy Future

(A science fiction romance mystery series set in future New Orleans)

Core Punch (1.0)

Sucker Punch (2.0)

One Two Punch: An Uneasy Future Bundle

Short Story Collections

Project Enterprise: The Short Stories

Do Wah Diddy Delete

Let's Fall in Love

The Real Dragon and other short stories

ABOUT THE AUTHOR

Award-winning, *USA Today* Bestselling author Pauline never liked reality, so she writes books. She likes to wander among the genres, rampaging like Godzilla, because she does love peril mixed in her romance.

To find out more about Pauline or her books:
http://paulinebjones.com

ISBN: 978-1-942583-64-6

❀ Created with Vellum

www.ingramcontent.com/pod-product-compliance
Lightning Source LLC
Chambersburg PA
CBHW060353180626
46817CB00008B/2989